The Forever Kind

KOKO HEART

Twatface forever!
All my love
Koko ♡

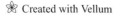 Created with Vellum

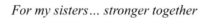

For my sisters… stronger together

Prologue

CLEO

My grin probably makes me look like a maniac but I don't care. Nothing can wipe it off my face as I stroll through my Uni's campus. Not even the curious stares from my fellow students. If anything, their reactions broaden my smile even more. I know they're probably labelling me as the weird one, grinning like the Cheshire cat as I make my way to lessons, but again I don't care. I love it here. I love the freedom I have to just be me. I miss Connor—my best friend, my brother from another mother—and I miss my sisters, but I also love just being me. Not one of the Cooper sisters, not Connor's sidekick. Just me, Cleopatra Cooper.

Of course, no one here calls me Cleopatra. It's Cleo all the way. I wasn't making the same mistake twice. I started school off as Cleopatra and had to fight my way through to be known as Cleo. Nope, not doing that again. Cleo, I can deal with. Cleopatra's too much.

But that's exactly how I'd describe my parents for bestowing that insane moniker on me in the first place. I get they're Shakespeare fanatics and named us all after his characters, but come on. Cleopatra? My mum did me dirty there. She tries to justify it by blaming her choice on my dark hair and dark eyes at birth. She claims it was the only name she could've chosen. I disagree completely, but it's a pointless argument as I still ended up being named after an Egyptian Queen.

My sisters are all blonde-haired, blue-eyed beauties like my mum, but I came out with black hair and eyes so dark they could pass for black, just like my dad. My features are the same as my sisters' though, which really throws people off sometimes.

Growing up I was the odd one out. Neighbours watched the trio of blonde children running after my equally blonde mother down the street, and then me, my dark hair flowing behind me, as I caught up to them. People always looked at me strangely, asked my mum 'is that one yours too?' But it never bothered me because I had my sisters.. We're as close as four sisters can be. We went everywhere together, and when we got a little bit older, found boyfriends and friends, we would still come together at the end of the week for sister time.

"Yo Cleo, where's that boyfriend of yours? We have training in a bit."

I turn and smile at Harry, my boyfriend's best friend and our flatmate. "I have no idea. I was supposed to be in class now, but it was cancelled at the last minute. I'll phone him in a bit, but I doubt he'll miss football training. He still believes he'll make it professionally."

I roll my eyes and chuckle as I think about Alex and his eternal optimism that he'll become a professional footballer. He plays for the university team but is nowhere near as good as he thinks he is. We've had a few arguments over it in our seven months of dating. I have a sarcastic, sassy approach to life and he's a bit sensitive about everything—especially his footballing abilities. Or lack of.

He's an okay guy. He treats me nicely and tells me he

loves me all the time. He's sweet, but very concerned with how things look to the outside world. He wants to *appear* to be the perfect boyfriend when in reality his listening skills are seriously below par. We aren't a couple you'd see in a Lucy Score book, with a beautifully written story full of conflict and resolution, who are ridiculously happy and devoted to each other. But I think we're happy in our own way.

"The boy's delusional. I don't know what you see in him, Cleo. Dump him and let me take you out. You know I'll show you a good time." Harry winks at me and gives me a smouldering look that he's perfected by practising it in the mirror. I know because I caught him. This is what happens when you flat share with guys in halls of residence.

"I'm sure you would, H, but you'd also be showing every other girl on campus that same good time, wouldn't you? I don't need to be catching anything from you now, do I?" I say through my chuckle.

His eyes twinkle and he grins at me mischievously. "I can assure you, baby, I'm as safe as can be. I know how to wrap up the goods. But come on, Cleo, I can't stay with just one woman. You can't put a cap on all this. " He swipes his hands over his impressively sculpted body, then pulls his shirt up and flashes his abs at me. He winks at me again and tells me, "If you change your mind, I'm just down the hall."

As he embraces me in a hug, a bubble of laughter erupts from me. With a kiss to my cheek, he sprints off in the opposite direction. I really like Harry, but there's no way in hell I'd date him. He's the very definition of a man-whore. Sometimes it's like Piccadilly circus with the endless stream of women coming and going in our place. He is fit though. Tanned olive skin, sexy stubble that goes on for days, and don't get me started on his thighs, or should I say tree trunks. I've always had a thing for footballers because of their impressive thighs.

Unfortunately, Alex definitely doesn't have that 'footballer' physique Harry has. But he also isn't a man-whore. It's one of the reasons I finally agreed to go out with him. He was a safe option. We've slotted into campus life and our relationship easily. Apart from a few arguments—mainly about me not caring what other people think and him caring a lot—we've been happy. We spend a lot of time together, living together will do that but it's been fun.

As I head down the hall in our flat, I silently pray our other flatmate Lacy isn't home. She isn't the friendliest of people. I've tried to be nice to her, but most of the time I just avoid her. I don't want to argue with anyone here and I really don't think she'd understand my snarky ways. She isn't a bad flatmate. She keeps the communal living spaces clean and tidy, but she's also very snobby. She looks like a goddamn supermodel with legs that go on for miles. She dresses like one too. And she likes to look down her nose at my dark clothes and grubby trainers. I dress for me and for my comfort, not because I'm following the latest trends. That's another thing that's caused rows between Alex and I, but I refuse to change who I am for anyone.

I open the door to Alex's room, ready to see why he's late for training and let my bag fall to my feet. Rage and humiliation engulf me at the sight I'm met with.

"Are you fucking kidding me right now?"

I stare at Alex's pasty white arse scrambling to get up and off our equally naked flatmate. Wave after wave of embarrassment and anger wash over me.

"Cleo, babe, it's not. I didn't. I'm sorry." Alex stutters out as Lacy very slowly picks up her clothes to get dressed.

"So let's get this straight, Alex. You didn't just fuck our flatmate behind my back, but you did it in the bed we sleep in as well? What kind of person fucking does that?" I screech at him. He stutters as he grabs his jeans off the floor and shoves

4

them on as Lacy, who's thrown on her little polka dot dress, walks toward me.

I clench my hands into fists ready to throat punch her—a skill my sisters taught me at a very young age. She may tower over my five-foot frame, but I can take this bitch down if I have to. You don't have Emilia Cooper as a sister and not learn how to fight. My sister is a badass, and she taught me everything I know.

She saunters over to me with her hands up in surrender and casually tells me, "I just want to leave, Cleo, not fight. *He* certainly isn't worth ruining my face over." She throws a disparaging look at Alex and motions for the door. I step out of her way as she walks out of the room and closes the door behind her. My main issue is with Alex afterall. I'll deal with Lacy later.

I turn to Alex as he steps closer to me, but I hold my hand up to stop him. I don't want to get expelled for beating the shit out of this fucker, but I will do exactly that if he tries to touch me right now.

"Cleo, she's been coming onto me for months. Flirting with me, trying to get me in bed. I finally slipped." He tries to explain to me, panic written all over his face.

I laugh and shake my head at his ridiculousness. "What, you slipped and your dick accidentally fell into her pussy? Seriously? I don't care if she was coming onto you. I couldn't care less if she laid herself out naked and served herself to you on a platter. *She* wasn't dating me. *She* has no one to remain faithful to. *She's* single.

"You, on the other hand, *you* committed yourself to me. *You* bloody chased me. Asked me out and told me you loved me. Why would you do that if you wanted to screw other people?" I fold my arms over my chest so he can't see them shaking. Hurt, betrayal, and anger dance around inside me, and I don't want him to see any of it. He lost the right to see my emotions the minute he cheated on me.

"I don't know, Cleo. Honestly, you're pretty and all but, fuck, you're mean. You don't believe in my dreams and always make fun of me for even having them. You make me feel stupid and never want to spend time with me. I swear you should've been born a bloke. You're not built for relation-ships. You're the kind of girl who enjoys being on her own too much to have a boyfriend. Everything came before me in your life. School, your family, your friends. I was always last on your list."

I fight the tears threatening to spill down my cheeks. I can't argue with anything he's saying. It's all true. I'm just about to apologise to him but he carries on. "You've never appreciated my romantic gestures AND you're so stubborn. You wouldn't change anything about yourself for me. Plus, come on, Cleo, Lacy's gorgeous. I'd be fucking mad to say no to that. You're so small. It's like walking around with a twelve year old under my arm."

My eyes open in sheer disbelief at the words coming out of his mouth. No less than two days ago he was telling me he loved me, and that I was the most beautiful girl he'd ever seen. I'm such an idiot. I was actually considering apolo-gising to this motherfucker as he did have a point about everything coming before him. But now, I'm not the slightest bit sorry. No, now I'm really pissed off.

I shake my head at my sheer stupidity. "Oh Alex, if you thought I was mean before, you're definitely not going to like what I'm about to say to you now." I stand straighter and pull my shoulders back. Smiling sweetly at him, I feel triumphant when I see fear flash through his eyes, and I go in for the kill. "You're a spoiled, uptight, delusional, little boy who couldn't find a G spot if I drew you a map." His eyes snap to me and I nod my head sadly at him as I

6

continue. "I accepted you had a smaller than average dick because I'm a firm believer it's not the size of the boat that matters but the motion in the ocean. Unfortunately, you disproved that theory on every occasion. I figured eventually you might find my clit and make some magic happen that way, but that never happened either. Every time we had sex, I had to finish the job you started because you're useless."

I pause to take a breath, he makes a weird little noise in his throat and asks me disbelievingly, "You're just saying that because you're hurt right?"

I huff out a bitter laugh at him, "Oh no, honey, I'm not. I'm being deadly serious. You may think I look like a kid because of my height, but you still fuck like you're a fifteen year old boy. It's really frustrating. Oh, and, I'm not hurt. I'm just annoyed I turned H down earlier today. I'm certain he would know how to make me scream for real. He's better on the pitch than you, so I'm sure he'd be better in bed too!"

His face turns a nice shade of red, embarrassment and anger emanating from him, and I allow a smug smile to creep over my lips as he hisses, "You wouldn't dare. Harry's my teammate."

I shrug my shoulders and look at him with big innocent eyes, "Would that upset you? Me, sleeping with your teammate. Maybe I'll make my way through the whole damn team whilst screaming, 'Yes. You fuck way better than Alex ever did,' to each and every one of them."

"Fuck you! You wouldn't dare." He shouts loudly, his eyes flashing fear and panic.

I slowly bend down, retrieve my bag and grab the door handle. I turn to look back and triumphantly raise my eyebrow at him, smirking right before I walk out and slam the door in his face. I head quickly down the hall and enter my room. I grab my desk chair and prop it under the door handle, just in case Lacy or Alex are stupid enough to try to come here anytime soon.

Alone, I let my tears fall. How could I be so fucking stupid? He was so relentless in chasing me I actually believed he did want me as badly as he pretended to. What an absolute joke. I should've stayed single. I've never been one to believe in happily ever after and fairy tales, that was always my younger sister Juliet's job. I wasn't stupid enough to think this was the next great love story. I didn't think we were made for each other. I honestly don't know if I believe that there's one person out there for you, but I had hoped this would've been something more worthwhile of my time and energy.

But nope, I chose a fucking cheater to be my first boyfriend. Well, never again. Looking over to my bed, I spot the little teddy bear he gave me. I reach out for it and squeeze its belly. Alex's voice rings out, "I love you, Cleo, always babe. Mwah." With tears streaming down my face I throw it across the room. This fucking bear should've been a giant red flag. I'm not the teddy bear loving kind of girlfriend, but Alex thought I should be.

Fucking teddy. Fucking Alex. He humiliated me. Paraded around campus with me, pretending to be madly in love with me, then he does this. Is this the first time? Have there been others? Did H know? Is everyone laughing at me behind my back?

My phone rings from my bag, distracting me from the humiliation. I know it's one of my sisters on the other end. The Cooper circle of comfort doesn't stop because I'm in uni. I stay seated, letting the phone go silent. A deluge of text messages ping in the stillness of my dorm room. I refuse to speak to them. They're the best people in the world but I don't want them to know I was stupid enough to fall for a fucktwat like Alex. Nell's in love with her soulmate Steve,

Juliet has this weird thing going on with Connor, and Emilia doesn't need anyone. I don't want to admit to choosing someone like Alex and having them know how stupid and naive I was to believe his lies. Embarrassment is one thing to face at uni, but going home and feeling it too? No thanks. This is one of those cases where it's better to keep the humiliation levels to a bare minimum.

~

I tap my fingernail on the desk whilst the administrator checks the system. "Sorry, there aren't any places available mid-term. You'll either have to rent privately off campus or stick it out where you are."

Stick it out where I am? Does she realise the amount of strength it's taken these past couple of days to not annihilate Lacy or Alex? I may have put a few shrimps in her bedpost and I definitely may have added hair dye to her shampoo and conditioner, her normal blonde locks are now a lovely shade of purple but the bitch still looks good. It's been torture. Seeing her prancing around campus and getting compliments on her hair. I want to rip each strand of it out with her smug, perfect, stupid smile. A frustrated growl leaves my throat as I turn around and crash straight into a redheaded bombshell I recognise from the majority of my classes.

"Sorry, Verity." I mumble to her.

She grabs my shoulders and lowers her face so she's looking into my eyes. "Cleo, are you alright? I heard about Alex and that skank. What kind of arseholes do that and then brag about it around campus? Absolutely no class at all." She lets my shoulders go.

I sigh and really take her in. She exudes confidence and wealth but has the kindest eyes.

"It's fine. Humiliating, but fine. SHE won't let me swap

to a different flat in halls." I glare back at the administrator who's completely ignoring me whilst clacking her nails on her keyboard.

"It's not fine and you shouldn't feel humiliated. But this is actually perfect. I need a flatmate. I live off campus. You wouldn't have to deal with the gossip as much. My mother and father are really wealthy, like obscenely wealthy. It's sickening. They bought me an apartment around the corner, but money can't buy friendship. And I'm lonely. Come live with me."

I look at her incredulously. Is she for real? We barely know each other. Her shining eyes are telling me she is, though, and I laugh. I laugh at the absurdity of it all. And at my stupid luck.

"Why not. Sign me up."

She squeals as she hugs me tightly and I squirm out of her grip.

"Ah, not a hugger, eh? That's fine, I can rein it in. I promise, as your new flatmate, to never sleep with your boyfriend, Cleo."

I roll my eyes at her as she links my arm in hers and we exit the building.

"I won't be getting another boyfriend, so you don't have to worry."

She turns her shocked face to me and asks, "But what about sex? You can't go without sex, Cleo. It's unnatural for someone as cute as you to go without sex."

Laughing, I tell her, "You don't need a boyfriend to have sex, Verity. Just a boy that's friendly. And I know plenty of friendly boys, starting with the university football team."

She cackles loudly and informs me, "Oh Cleo, I like you. We'll get along fabulously. Alex is on the team isn't he?"

I grin at her mischievously, "Yep."

She cackles again and I already feel better being around her.

"Who knows, Cleo. Maybe you'll fall in love with his best friend and teammate. That would piss him off."

I chuckle at her as a longing for my sister Juliet washes over me, but I shut it down. I can handle this on my own. And maybe with a little help from my new flatmate. "Er, nope. Made the mistake of dating a 'footballer' before, I won't do that again."

CHAPTER 1

Stupid Juliet. Stupid Connor. Stupid Verity. And stupid bloody Jean-Pierre.

I stomp out of my office after being railroaded by love's young fuckwits, Connor and Juliet. They forced me into taking the biggest contract my company has ever seen, and whilst I should be grateful, it pushes me so far out of my comfort zone it's unreal. On the plus side, Juliet and Connor look like they're getting on better. Maybe my misery will help bring them together again.

Jumping into the taxi I just hailed, I slam the door angrily and tell the driver the address of the restaurant I'm heading to.

"Jeez lady, you nearly took my door off the hinges then. What's got you so riled up? Little slip of thing, didn't think you had it in you." He chuckles at his own wit and I roll my eyes at him, turning my body toward the window, silently cursing Verity for landing this shitshow on me. She was supposed to be here dealing with this, but no, she fell in love and is now swanning around Europe with her rich, model boyfriend. She doesn't know when she'll be back in the 'real world' of going to work and helping run the company she started with her best friend.

My phone rings and I grab it out of my bag to see Verity's name flash across the screen. I swipe the call open and fight the smile that wants to tweak my lips upwards when I see my beautiful best friend on a video call.

"Your ears must be burning because I was just cussing you out." I tell her, rolling my eyes when she starts laughing at me.

"Who to? Not the client, I hope. You need to be professional around him, sweetie." She sing-songs back to me, managing to ooze professionalism from her sunny getaway.

If I could, I'd frizz her hair up right now, but since she's on the phone I settle for blowing a raspberry at her.

"I was cussing you in my head. I'm in a cab, going to meet him now." I flip the camera so that she can see the driver and flip it back to me.

"This was your job, Verity. You're the professional lovey who deals with weddings and engagements and I'm the mean spirited, sarcastic boss bitch who deals with anything and everything corporate. Why did you leave me to deal with this? This guy has left me so many messages about the party I want to throttle him before I've even met him."

She chuckles at my whining and I catch the driver giving me a curious look in the rearview mirror. I throw back my best scowl and he averts his eyes to the road.

Gazing back at the screen, I can't help feeling envious of Verity. She's laying on a sun lounger wearing a giant floppy hat that would make anyone else look ridiculous, but makes Verity look the epitome of elegance and grace. Doubt flows through me as I rub my hand over my plain black trousers. I cast a glance at the little screen that shows my face, letting out a sigh. Thankfully, Verity misses it so I square my shoulders and focus back on what she's saying.

"Listen Cleo. I know you feel like I've abandoned you, and I have in a way. But it's all going to be good for you. You're more than capable of dealing with an engagement party, and the client is lovely. Once you meet him, face to face, you'll see just how lovely he is. Don't be put off by his eagerness to make this party amazing. Please? He's trusting us—well you—to do this justice for his best friend. Just think of the publicity. This could be it for our company, Cleo. Our vision could come true for Dream Team Events."

"I know, Verity, it's why I'm in the back of a black cab with a nosey driver," I say pointedly as I catch the driver turning his music down so he can listen to our conversation. He chuckles and I carry on talking.

"Isn't that weird though? Why is he arranging his best friend's engagement party? Shouldn't the bride be doing that? Or even the friends or family of the bride? Not the bloody best man. You can't tell me that's not odd, Verity." I argue back with her. Her laughter is starting to annoy me but is also making me miss my crazy best friend.

"I asked about that. Turn me down and put me up to your ear so I can whisper and the nosey driver doesn't hear please." When I do as she asks, the driver scoffs which makes me giggle at how invested he is in our conversation. "Am I quiet enough? Okay, good. The bride's schedule is really tight and she's filming constantly. She has exclusive rights with a magazine company for the engagement party pictures and doesn't want to take risks with voiding her contract with them. She's donating the fee to various children's charities, so it's imperative we keep everything top secret. She also adores Antony and thinks it's such a unique twist on a somewhat overdone concept. How many people can say the best man planned the engagement party?"

She's infuriating when she's smug and able to answer my frustrations with well thought out answers.

I turn the volume back up and tell her through gritted teeth, "Fine. I'll be professional and I'll try to be less judgy. I swear if this guy wasn't so well connected or one of Emilia's clients, I wouldn't have taken this job at all. It'll only be for a few months right?"

She laughs down the phone at me and I sigh back.

"We're pulling up outside the restaurant now anyway so I'll speak to you later. I'll try not to kill little Mr. Sunshine upon meeting him." She cackles down the line at me and blows me a kiss. I roll my eyes back in response and quickly say goodbye, cutting off another round of her giggles.

When I plop my phone into my bag and check how much my fare is, the driver catches my eye in the rearview mirror and tells me, "You go in there and knock his socks off, little Cleo. Be that boss bitch you said you were."

Smiling, I tap my bank card onto the payment machine. "You really are nosey, aren't you?"

He turns in his seat and grins at me, "So my wife says, yeah."

I laugh as I finish my payment, making sure I leave a rather generous tip for my very nosey cheerleader.

The breath whooshes out of me as I step inside the restaurant. It's so big and fancy here, I immediately feel like I don't fit in. Verity would fit in. Emilia would fit in. But me? Not even a little bit.

I'm no stranger to the 'fake it till you make it' mantra, so I stand straighter and flip my hair behind my shoulder, sucking up my concerns as I step forward to let the Maître'd know I'm meeting someone here. Apparently my party has already arrived, fifteen minutes early.

Mr. Sunshine's prompt. I don't know why that annoys me,

but it does. So far everything about him has annoyed me. His perky emails, his constant need to mention love in his messages, and the incessant need for reassurance that we'll do a good job. All of it. Dealing with people is one of the worst things about running an events company. If I just had to deal with the organisation aspect it would be a breeze, but nope, I have to have actual conversations with real life people. And that sucks.

Nerves gnaw at me as I'm escorted to my table. I glance around at the high domed ceilings, the elegant crystal chandeliers hanging from them and the gold dimmed light features on the walls setting a romantic and intimate ambience even though it's during the day. As we weave in between the decadent tables covered in white table cloths, I note the amount of cutlery on the table and roll my eyes. It's so unnecessary. But I suppose the suited and booted snobs sitting at the tables would disagree with me. I hope Mr. Sunshine isn't a pretentious twat but he's a footballer of course he is. I stand up straighter again, huff a breath out and channel Emilia, my most confident sister. As I approach our table, my breath catches in my throat as I gaze upon the most beautiful man I've ever laid eyes on. He stands to greet me, his hand held out for me to shake. I stare at him dumbfounded and reach my own hand out. As soon as our skin connects, a warmth spreads through me, sending heat right down to my toes. I grip his hand firmly and shake it, like I've been taught to do by my dad with any business associate. The difference with this one is I don't want this handshake to end.

I lick my lips and reluctantly let go. I sigh out the breath I didn't even realise I was holding. Shit! This man is sex on legs and I'm finding it difficult to remember why I'm here. Business, Cleo, strictly business, I remind myself in my head. No wonder Verity said I'd enjoy meeting him face to face. He's gorgeous.

He motions for me to sit with a carefree smile and a wave of his hand toward my chair. I do, eagerly, as my legs feel like jelly and I don't want him to know that. But judging from his grin I think he knows the effect he has on women.

He takes his place opposite me, and I use the few seconds I have to take him in. His eyes are the colour of whiskey with flecks of gold in them. His tanned olive skin looks smooth and delicious in the dimmed lights and I fight every urge I have to lean across the table and run my tongue over every inch of his skin to see if it tastes as good as it looks.

He smiles at me, flashing his dead straight, perfectly white teeth and a pink tinge creeps up onto my cheeks. What the actual fuck? I never blush. My sisters blush all the time because of their fair complexions, but I never do.

"It's so nice to meet you in person, Cleo. Although you're not what I was expecting," he smoothly tells me whilst picking up his glass of water and taking a sip.

What does he mean by that? Is he disappointed? Embarrassment surges through me and I bite my tongue, stopping me from saying, "Screw you, Mr. White teeth." Instead, I reply, "It's nice to meet you too, Mr. Marcello. I know originally you were dealing with my business partner, Verity, but as we've previously discussed via email, she's taken some well-deserved time off. I apologise if that wasn't clear in my *many* messages to you and you're disappointed she isn't here today."

I smile tightly at him and cross my legs under the table to try to ease the throb pulsing in my clit from just looking at this handsome specimen. My feelings are all confused and I don't like it one bit.

"You've misunderstood me, and I apologise for that. I knew I'd be meeting you. In fact, I was looking forward to it." He grins at me and licks his lips as I force my eyes to keep looking into his and not track the movement. "I was just shocked because you look so different to Emilia. I expected blonde hair and blue eyes—looks like an angel but is ruthless as the devil." He smiles this time, and I can't help but chuckle at his description of my big sister. I'm thankful I misunderstood his comment and he's not disappointed in seeing me. Not that I should care about his disappointment, this isn't a date.

"Yeah, that describes Emilia to a T. She and my sisters all rock the angel look well, whilst I give off queen of darkness vibes. We may look different but we definitely are sisters. She taught me everything she knows." I tilt my head and raise my eyebrow at him, daring him to question it.

He laughs and sits forward in his chair, resting his elbows on the table. "I have to say, I think the queen of darkness look is a much better one. I think you're absolutely stunning."

I clear my throat and smile at him, "Why, Mr. Marcello, you're not flirting with me are you? That would be highly unprofessional now, wouldn't it?"

He chuckles back at me and rubs his dark stubbled chin. I bite my bottom lip thinking of how it would feel to have that stubble running over my body. Especially between my thighs.

"I'm a professional on the pitch. Off the pitch I don't have to worry. If I see a beautiful woman, I should be allowed to tell her so. You are by the way, Cleo. Beautiful, that is. Am I okay to call you Cleo?"

I smirk and sit back in my chair. "Yes, Cleo is fine. Thank you for the compliment, but I think we should try to always remain professional, Mr. Marcello. We're here to discuss your best friend's engagement party, right?"

I pick up my glass of water and take a sip. My mouth is drier than the dessert after one little compliment from him and hearing my name on his lips. I really don't understand what's going on with my body right now. He's not the first attractive man I've seen, but he is the hottest. He looks like a combination of Michele Morrone and Sebastian Stan and my body is struggling to cope. His grin is full of mischief but his eyes tell me a different story. He may act cheeky, but there's a fire deep inside of him, waiting to burn me from the inside out if I want it to.

If we were meeting at a bar or club, not for business reasons, I'd already be heading home with him. But this is a business meeting. One that Emilia set up. One that could put my events company on the map. I cannot fuck this up because he's hotter than hell.

I clear my throat and place the glass down carefully, desperately trying not to let him see I'm rattled by him, and wait for him to respond.

"We are. I need something that screams originality but also shows just how much they love each other. They're two of the best people in the world and they've found true love. I think that should be celebrated. It's a rare thing to find in this day and age, Cleo, wouldn't you agree?" He stares into my eyes, optimism and hope shining in his.

I don't know how to reply. A part of me wants to unleash my snarky ways on him and let him know exactly what I think about 'true love', but the other part doesn't want to upset him. He genuinely looks so excited about his friends being in love and happy and I don't want to ruin that. What is wrong with me? Since when do I care about a stranger's feelings? I stranglehold the snarky reply trying to claw its way out of me, smile and nod my head as I respond, "Absolutely, Mr. Marcello. At Dream Team Events we strive to give our clients whatever they need. You tell me what you want and I'll deliver it."

A twinkle shines in his eyes and he grins at me again. "Hmmm really? This could be interesting, Cleo."

He's infuriatingly charming so while I don't stifle my eyeroll, I do give him a genuine smile at the same time. The way he keeps saying my name isn't helping my resolve either. It rolls off his tongue so easily and makes me question what else his tongue would be good at.

"Within reason, Mr. Marcello." His arrogant footballer personality shines through. It surprises me that instead of being irked by it, I'm pleasantly amused.

He frowns at me slightly and shakes his head. "Please call me, Antony, Cleo. Hey, I've just realised something." A huge grin spreads over his face, and I just know I'm going to hate what comes out of his mouth next, but I can't fight the grin that's taken residence on my face too. "I'm Antony and you're Cleo. Please tell me your full name is Cleopatra." It's my turn to frown. I clear my throat and reach up to twist the sunflower charm on my necklace as he lets out an appreciative laugh. "It is, isn't it? We're Antony and Cleopatra. Well how about that? This is meant to be Cleopatra." He raises his water glass and clinks it with mine.

I blow out an exasperated breath and tell him, "Look, my name is Cleopatra, but I prefer to be called Cleo, so let's stick to that please."

He looks at me with a confused look on his perfectly symmetrical face.

"Why? Cleopatra is an awesome name. It suits you perfectly."

Agitation flows through me but I'm still trying to rein in my queen of darkness, so through gritted teeth, I tell him, "I prefer to be called Cleo because I do, Antony. So how many people will be attending this party?"

I divert the conversation back onto neutral territory as the waiter approaches and takes our orders. I drink some more water and take the reprieve to try to calm down my attraction to him, but also my annoyance with him. Only I could be turned on and annoyed at the same damn time.

"I'm not sure of the overall number yet. Have you read

Antony and 'the name we aren't allowed to call you', before?" He asks me with a smirk and I don't know whether I want to reach over and smack him or kiss him.

I'm horny and irritated by this man.

"Yes, Antony. I have." I sigh out. "My parents are Shakespeare fanatics and taught English literature at professor levels. We are all named after Shakespearean characters and are extremely well versed in his works. Can we please start discussing the party details?"

He shakes his head at me and places his elbows on the table, resting his chin in his hands.

"We're setting the groundwork for our 'professional' relationship here Cleopa…" he abruptly stops. "Cleo."

I glare at him.

He smiles back and tells me, "Whoops, sorry. We'll be working very closely together for the next few months and we need to be in sync with each other if we're to pull off the party of the year. Get used to me, Cleopatra, you'll be seeing a lot of your Antony."

"You're an odd person, do you know that?" I coolly tell him, expecting to see him flinch back as I glare at him.

He grins inanely at me, "I do. You'll come to love my brand of oddness soon enough, Cleopatra."

I grunt out a sigh of disapproval but don't correct him again as the waiter places our food in front of us. I can't help the smirk on my lips when I glance at him and he winks at me, flashing that million pound smile.

He's so annoying. I think I might be in trouble with this one.

CHAPTER 2

Antony

I'm driving back to my house in Hampstead with a grin as wide as the Cheshire Cat's. Snippets of my 'meeting' with Cleopatra flash through my mind and turn my grin into a full on smile. Cleopatra Cooper is definitely my cup of tea. She's beautiful, sarcastic, hard and soft at the same time. I picture her face, her beautiful pouty lips, her little button nose, and those eyes. They were wildly luminous considering how dark they were. There was a blankness in them though, like she was keeping them guarded. And I want to know why.

The bridal march song I set as my best friend Charlie's ringtone interrupts my thoughts. I know he's dying to know how it went today. I pull over and switch my electric Porsche Macan off and accept the video call. "Ciao, Charlie?"

"Why are you so smiley and speaking to me in Italian?" he shoots back to me. Suspicion ripe on his face.

I feel my smile get wider. "The party planner. I think I'm in love. *Lei é perfetta.*"

I watch as he smacks his forehead with the palm of his hand.

"You have got to be kidding me, Antony. You think they're all perfect. Last month you were in love with the physio. The month before that it was the delivery girl bringing us our sandwiches. You have a problem. A serious fucking problem."

I frown at him and shake my head in protest but realise he's right. I have used these words before. This time is different though. I don't say that to him because I've said that before as well.

Instead, I chuckle and tell him, "When you meet her, you'll understand. You remember the description I told you when we were younger of what my ideal partner would be?"

He nods his head and sighs, "Yes, Antony. How can I forget? You've drummed it into my head. Even made me write it in a diary, a little girl's pink one with a tiny padlock and everything... Why am I still friends with you?"

Laughing, I tell him, "Because I'm fucking awesome and you know it. Anyway, tell me who I described."

He sighs and rolls his eyes as he regales me with information I already know.

"Your ideal partner is someone who is feisty but loving. Someone who is kind but strong. Someone who is goal orientated—successful in her own right so she doesn't have to rely on you, but could if she wanted to. You'd like her to be petite with dark hair—you're not opposed to blondes but prefer brunettes. You don't want a typical WAG, but you do want someone who'll support you in everything you do. You'd prefer someone who doesn't care about designer clothes and materialistic things. Ultimately you'd want someone you can forge a partnership with like your mum and dad have. If she's named Cleopatra it's a bonus. You want the forever kind of love not the fleeting kind. Did I get it all?"

I nod my head at him, a smug smile plastered on my face. "You did, and you just described Cleo, short for Cleopatra, to a T. How about that? Antony and Cleopatra."

"Okay, that's pretty awesome considering who your

parents are and everything, but you've met her once. If you genuinely like her, don't do your normal routine of thinking you're in love straight away. You always end up hurt, and I don't want you to get hurt again." He grabs the back of his neck, clearly awkward at this exchange.

I smile back reassuringly. "It's okay, man. I'll go into this with my eyes wide open, I promise. But come on, Antony and Cleopatra. Mama and Papa will flip at this." I grin as I think about my mama's reaction. I was named after my papa—Antony senior—and my mama was named after a very famous queen of Egypt—Cleopatra—but she goes by the name Patti. They were destined to be, like their namesakes all those years ago, and so are we. I know it.

"Jeez, you have that weird far off look in your eyes you get when you picture your happily ever after. You're not going to listen to me at all are you? You're going to dive straight in, head first, again." Shaking his head at me as I laugh, he blows out an exasperated breath and then grins.

"I promise I won't let anything affect my game, Charlie. And I promise I'll proceed with caution with Cleo. I want her to throw you and Zoe a kickarse party, that's my priority. But if I can wrangle her to go out with me and fall head over heels in love, I won't turn that down either." I grin and flutter my eyelashes at him.

"Idiot. Absolute fucking idiot. It's a good job I like your old man, Antony. Otherwise I'd have cut you loose as a friend a long time ago."

He grins at me and leans back in his chair.

"No, you wouldn't. You love me just as much as you love my mama and papa. Stop lying to yourself or I'll phone Zoe up and tell her you're being mean to me. You know she'll take my word over yours. She loves me more than she loves you, Bro."

I chuckle as he sticks his middle finger up at me. "Sometimes I think she does. Seriously, tread carefully and keep me updated. I swear being friends with you has aged me over the years."

"Hmm, I think I can see a few grey hairs to be honest," I tell him, and laugh as he swears and hangs up on me.

Before I throw my phone onto the front seat, I bring up Cleo's name and type out a text message to her.

Me: Cleopatra, I have a few ideas I'd like to run by you? When are you free next?

Cleopatra: Maybe you should have done that over our lunch meeting instead of spending the duration of it winding me up by calling me Cleopatra.

Me: But where's the fun in that? You need to relax a little, Cleopatra.

Cleopatra: For the love of… Would you prefer a working lunch meeting again or something else?

Me: I like professional Cleopatra (winking emoji)

Cleopatra: (Eye roll emoji)

Me: Fine. We've had lunch already. How about dinner?

Cleopatra: A working dinner?

Me: You're boring. Yes, a working dinner.

Cleopatra: (Laughing emoji) You're the oddest man I've ever met.

Me: I told you before, you'll come to love my brand of odd. Tomorrow night, be ready at six. I'll pick you up.

Cleopatra: You don't know where I live. I'll meet you at the restaurant.

Me: Whose fault is that?

Cleopatra: I've just met you, I'm not going to tell you my address.

Me: Fine, you're right I guess, even if you are frustrating.

Cleopatra: *I'M* frustrating? Pot, kettle, black…

Me: See you tomorrow, Cleopatra.

Cleopatra: (Eyeroll emoji)

Happy with our arrangement for a not-date, I throw my phone onto the passenger seat, turn the music up loud and sing my heart out. Cleopatra Cooper has definitely brightened up my day with her queen of darkness routine, and I'm not afraid to say I'm a little bit taken with her.

CHAPTER 3
Cleo

Flinging my shoes onto the floor I call out to Juliet, "Princess, you home?"

Nothing. She must be with Emilia and Marcus. Or hopefully with Connor. She agreed to work with him today, which is a step in the right direction for those two.

I heave a sigh out and look around my empty apartment. I haven't been alone here for a long time. Between Verity and Jean-Pierre and then Juliet moving in, it's always been busy. It's oddly quiet and I'm finding it a bit disconcerting.

Music. I need music.

I grab my phone from my bag, laptop from the kitchen counter, and head over to the sofa. Whilst the laptop is loading, I choose an old school RnB playlist from my phone. With the music blaring, I head into the kitchen to pour myself a big glass of wine. God knows I deserve it after the day I've had.

I settle on the sofa and bring up the document I was working on earlier. The one titled 'Antony's party.' Instead of scoping out venues like I'm supposed to be doing, I bring google up and search for him instead. I shouldn't be doing this. I want to though. I want to see more of this annoying but delicious man.

A plethora of images appear before my eyes. Antony in a football kit. Yuck. Antony in an England jersey. Meh. Antony playing football—his thighs are a beautiful sight to behold. Antony shirtless, wow! Shirtless Antony might just be my new favourite thing in the whole damn world. And that irritates the life out of me. Fuck, he's ripped. His abs have abs. And do not even get me started on his damn thighs. Lust shoots through me and the throbbing in my clit starts up again.

I slam the laptop closed and gulp at my wine. Nope, I'm not going to do it. I will not paddle the pink canoe to Antony Marcello. He's a client and a footballer. Not happening. There will be no finger painting tonight. Thank you very much.

I grab my phone and wine and head into the bathroom. Maybe a cold shower will calm my wanting libido down. Devouring the last of my wine, I place the empty glass on the side next to the sink. I turn the music up louder, step into the water and scream. Fuck that. I switch the heat up and let the hot water run over my body and soothe the chills away.

Fucking Antony. My mind takes those two words and conjures up an image of me fucking Antony and I bite on my lip as the throb starts up again. Images of his strong muscular thighs and his sculpted chest flash through my mind and I groan out loud as my hand brushes over my pebbled nipple. No! I wrench my hand from my breast and place it firmly on the tile in front of me. I will not think of Antony whilst having a ménage a moi. I'll picture other celebrities, as far from Antony as I can think of. Charlie Hunnam, blond hair and blue eyed. He'll do nicely. I place my forehead on the tiled wall and let my hand graze over my breasts, imagining him touching me. The throb gets stronger as an image of him smiling at me flashes in my mind but quickly changes to Antony winking at me.

"Gah! Fuck off out of my brain, Antony. I don't like footballers. I want motorcycle heroes." I shout into the cascading water. I close my eyes again and take a deep breath.

Charlie. I'm in the shower with Charlie. Not Antony the footballer, but Charlie with his tattoos and blond beard. My hand slips over my wet skin and I groan as I roll my nipple with my thumb and forefinger. I pinch a little harder and moan. I can't stop. I need this release. I imagine the water running down his body, over the grooves of his chiselled abs. I trace the trickles with my tongue. He groans in pleasure as I wrap my hand around his dick. I lift my head to see the ecstasy etched on his face and gasp when I see whiskey coloured eyes looking back at me instead of blue. I watch as perfectly straight, white teeth bite into very pink full lips and droplets of water fall onto tanned olive skin.

I give in.

I can't fight this anymore.

I let my brain conjure up whatever images it wants to and sigh when Antony is what it wants. His head lowers and he takes my nipple in his mouth. He twirls his tongue around it and I cry out in ecstasy as his hand lowers and slides onto my pussy. The throb intensifies as he kisses my neck and plunges his fingers inside of me. "Cleopatra," he moans out. Up and down my hand moves over his shaft and he grunts his approval. He thrusts his fingers in and out of my core and places his thumb on my clit and my whole body explodes into a colourful burst of pure bliss as 'Antony' slips out of my mouth.

I take a few deep breaths to calm my rapid heart rate and slide down the shower wall until I'm sitting on the floor, water still pounding on me, my legs unable to stand any longer. Shit. That was a fucking intense orgasm to my business associate. Dammit.

I grab a hair tie from the vanity top and tie off the end of my french braid. Tomorrow will be a curly hair day. I reach for the phone and turn the music off, stomping out of the bathroom ready for some food, but the silence in my apartment is odd. Where is Juliet? I pull up our family group chat and type out a message.

Me: SOS. Has anyone seen Princess?
Nell: Isn't she at your place?
Me: (Eyeroll emoji) We aren't playing fucking hide and seek, Nell.
Emilia: Someone is feisty tonight.
Nell: RUDE!
Me: Sorry. Just had a stressful day.
Juliet: I'm out with Emilia. Are you okay?
Connor: Was it that bad?
Nell: Was what that bad?
Me: Nothing. Just a difficult client. It's fine. I was just wondering where she was. I should've just messaged her.
Nell: Are we annoying you already?
Emilia: Did you need to ask that, Sis?
Juliet: Want me to come home?
Marcus: Cleo, baby girl. What's the matter? Tell Uncle Marcus.
Me: I'm fine, just hungry. Princess, stay where you are. Have fun. I'm going to order some food and head to bed.
Emilia: Loosely translated to 'leave her the fuck alone and let her relax and deal with her bad mood on her own.' We're all looking at you, Nell.

Nell: I can't help but want to look after you all, Emilia. I will leave you be though, Cleo. We love you.

I smile at my crazy family but don't respond. I love them all so much, but they do drive me mad a majority of the time. We are so involved in each other's lives I sometimes question whether it's healthy or not. But I wouldn't change it for anything.

Just as I'm about to open the food app to order something to eat, my phone beeps in my hand and Antony's name flashes on the screen. A smile breaks out over my face. I quickly stop it and force a frown in its place. Not that it matters as he can't see me. And it's just a text. But I don't want to get a stupid smile over a text from him. He's just a client. A client I just had an orgasm over, but that's besides the point.

Antony: Cleopatra, I'm bored and can't decide what to eat. What are you having?

Me: Erm, why are you texting me about this?

Antony: I'm bored. I already told you.

Me: (Eyeroll emoji) but why me?

Antony: Because I like you, Cleopatra.

Me: You don't know me.

Antony: Who's fault is that? Tell me about yourself?

Me: No. You hired me to plan your party, not to be your friend.

Antony: So just be my friend because you want to.

I chuckle to myself even though I don't want to. There's just something about this man that seems to get under my skin. All day today I've been thinking about him, and each thought made me smile. I don't get all goofy and grin over guys, especially not professional footballers. That's not me.

32

Normally I'd have told any other person to fuck off by now, but with him, I want to dive into the rabbit hole and see what being his 'friend' would be like. My fingers type a response to him as if they've been doing it all of their life.

Me: Chinese food. It's my favourite. There, that's enough friendliness for tonight, I think.
Antony: Interesting. What are you ordering specifically though?
Me: (Eye roll emoji) an egg fried rice, sweet and sour chicken balls, crispy seaweed and prawn crackers. Do you want me to tell you what I had for breakfast too seeing as you already know what I had for lunch?
Antony: If you want to, sure. I'm open to knowing everything about you, Cleopatra.
Me:..
Antony: Okay, what's your address?
Me: I'm NOT telling you my address. Stalker alert!
Antony: That's rude, Cleopatra. I'm not a stalker. I was going to order food for you from this amazing place, but because of your snarky queen of darkness attitude, you can pay for your own food.
Me: Oh no, what an inconvenience. Because I haven't been paying for my own food for a long time now, have I?
Me: That was sarcasm, in case you missed it.
Antony: You get hangry. That's amusing. I'll see you tomorrow for dinner, Cleopatra. Goodnight.

What the actual fuck just happened? I do not get hangry. I don't need him to order me food. And I don't need him to pay for it either. It was a nice gesture though. Shaking my head, I pull up the food app and place my order.

I sigh as I open the laptop and come face to face with the search for Antony Marcello again. I scan over the images and deliberately ignore the ones with his body on show. I come across a few of him with various beautiful women. Tall, blonde, model-like women that look a lot like older versions of Lacy, my old flatmate.

Anger rises up in my throat.

"Stupid, fucking twatface. That's your new name now." I tell the computer screen. Not able to deal with the emotion surging through me, and knowing it's completely irrational to feel this way after meeting him once, I reach over for my phone and change his name from Antony to Twatface. It may be a petty move, but it calms the anger and hurt from old wounds and replaces it with a sense of satisfaction.

I close the search down and instead start looking at venues, which I should have been doing earlier instead of jilling off in the shower and trying to be his friend over text. Professionalism is key here because, as I remind myself for the millionth time today and hope it starts to sink into my brain, he *is* a client. And a damn footballer.

CHAPTER 4
Antony

As I sit down on the bench in our locker room, wrapped in a towel and fresh from a shower, I smile as an image of Cleopatra flits through my mind.

"Oi Marcello, what's got you grinning like a looney toon?" Lockheart, one of my teammates shouts over to me.

"What's a looney toon, old timer?" Brady, the young American asks as his towel falls dangerously low on his hips.

"You're so fucking young, newbie. And pull your God damn towel up. None of us want to see your junk when it falls down. Save that for your fucking TikGram shit you do." Lockheart scolds him but Brady just grins and wiggles his hips in front of him.

As Lockheart, our oldest and longest serving player, takes a swipe at him, Brady jumps back and spins on his heels to face me. "Anyway, Stallion, what's got you smiling like that? You got a little hottie keeping you up all night long? Is that why y'all are so tired? Or is it because y'all old as fuck?"

I look up at him and smirk, "Wouldn't you like to know."

He grins back, a twinkle in his blue eyes. "Hell yeah, I would. You getting some without telling us? We're your bruh's, your teammates."

I roll my eyes at him, which immediately makes me think of Cleopatra, and that causes me to smile harder.

Charlie, our team captain, walks in and claps Brady on the shoulder and tells him, "Teammates? You've only played a handful of games, newbie."

Lockheart and a few others who've joined us in the changing room laugh as Brady frowns at me. "That's because your boy over there won't stop hogging the limelight."

I chuckle at him and shake my head, "Your time will come, whippersnapper. One day I'll be too old to kick a ball and then you'll get your shot."

He grumbles something about me already being too old, but I know it's all in jest with him. He's just desperate to get on the pitch for longer than a few minutes at a time but he has to earn that right.

Charlie approaches me, half dressed and spraying deodorant as he comes. "What have you got planned today? Are you meeting with Cleopatra?"

I nod my head and grab his deodorant, spraying some on myself as he frowns at me. Charlie's been my best friend since we were kids. We joined Heath Hampstead FC together. We were even roommates at one stage, but he abandoned me to live with Zoe. I can't blame him. She's the best, and she smells a lot better than I do. With or without his deodorant.

"Yeah, we're having a 'working' dinner tonight. Don't worry, I'll still plan you the best party, dude, but I'll do it whilst wooing Cleopatra too." I grin at him, grabbing my clothes to get dressed.

He shakes his head and points his finger at me. "I still think you should proceed with caution. She's working for you. She's Emilia—AKA, Shark's—sister. If it all goes wrong, she'll rip your bollocks off, mate."

A frown mars my face as I pull my jumper over my head.

I didn't think about Emilia and the complications chasing Cleopatra could cause.

"Do you think I need to talk to Emilia first? Like ask her permission or something? I mean, she's my agent, she controls everything. She could get me sold to another team or advertising hemorrhoid cream or something if this goes tits-up."

Charlie laughs at the very idea and I push him as all the other guys turn and shout, "fight." I roll my eyes at all of them shaking my head as I yell, "Shut the fuck up. We aren't on the youth team. Idiots." Chuckles filter through from them as they go back to getting ready.

Charlie turns to me, shaking his head. "You're the idiot. You don't have to ask Emilia's permission, she isn't her sister's keeper for God sakes. Maybe talk to her about her though. You could learn some things from her. See if Cleopatra is actually a good fit for you before you propose and name the kids you'll have with her."

I sheepishly look at him as I place my wallet and keys into my pocket.

He slaps his forehead and chuckles, "You've already named your kids haven't you? You've pictured your proposal and everything. What is wrong with you?"

I shrug and tell him, "Nothings wrong with me. And I haven't named our kids per say, just my kids. I like to be prepared." He laughs openly at me and I grin back at him knowing that even though he calls me crazy and gets annoyed with me on a daily basis, he loves me and has my back like no other.

"Where are you headed now?" He asks as we throw our jackets on and head out of the changing room. The training grounds are filled with staff and players loitering around. Our coach is working with a few players on the pitch and waves out to us.

"I'm paying a visit to Shark." I wiggle my eyebrows at him. We walk out into the car park and I'm shocked to see Brady arguing with a curvy pretty redhead over by his car. I tap Charlie's shoulder and jerk my head for him to look where I am. "Everything okay, Brady?" I shout over to him.

The young girl's face glows a glorious shade of red but she turns away from Brady and tells us, "Brady, as you call him, is acting like a dick and being territorial and possessive over me even though he is *just my friend*." She turns back to Brady as confusion, anger and worry sweep over his features, and tells him, "I'll talk to whomever I want to talk to, buddy. And *if* I want to date one of your teammates, I will. Understand, Jaxson Brady?" She spins on her heel, storms over to a little red Mini Cooper, jumps into the driver's side and speeds out of the car park.

We both turn to look at Brady as he shouts, "Fuck!" into the air whilst tugging on the ends of his curly blonde hair, before he quickly jumps into his car and hightails it after her.

I scratch my head as Charlie whistles. "I didn't realise you could be in the dog house with someone when you're not even with them. Shit, poor Brady."

I nod my head at him. "I wonder who asked her out? She said teammate. Probably Lockheart winding him up, no?" He nods at me as I open the door to my car and hop inside. "I'll let you know how it goes with Shark, and with Cleopatra later too. Wish me luck."

He laughs at me as he gets into his car, puts his seatbelt on and tells me, "Let's hope you walk away with your balls still intact. Good luck, Antony." Laughing, he pulls away. I stick my middle finger up at him even though I doubt he can see me. Made me feel better though.

∾

"Oh for the love of God… What do you want, Antony?"

Emilia stops in the doorway of her office and I chuckle at her abruptness. "That isn't a nice way to talk to one of your top clients, Shark. What is it with you Cooper sisters being mean?"

She chuckles at me and walks over to her desk, elegantly lowering herself into her chair. She looks immaculate as always. Her platinum hair is pinned back in a bun and the black shirt she's wearing is buttoned up to the collar. Ever the professional is Shark.

"I take it you met Cleo then? Plus, I've been your agent for years now. I'm entitled to say, "Oh for the love of God," when I see you sitting in a chair in my office unannounced. I've earned it." She smirks at me, sits forward in her chair and places her elbows on the desk, resting her hands under her chin. A total power move and one she's taught me to use on occasion. Emilia is fucking awesome.

"Fair enough, Shark. Are all of you mean, though? Is it like a genetic Cooper thing? Does it run through your veins or something?"

She rolls her eyes at me and I can't fight the grin from my face. "No, we aren't. Juliet and Nell are like rays of sunshine compared to Cleo and I. The only difference is, Cleo looks the part and I don't. The blonde hair makes people think I'm sweet and innocent. Ha!" She raises an eyebrow at me and laughs at my hands held up in surrender, letting her know I'm not one of those stupid people.

I'd never underestimate Emilia Cooper, she isn't called Shark for nothing.

"Tell me about Cleopatra, please." I request, getting straight to the point.

As graceful as can be, Emilia leans back in her chair, grinning gleefully at me.

"Why Antony, do you have a thing for my little sister? This is fucking brilliant. What do you want to know?"

I breathe out a huge sigh of relief and ask her, "Is she single? Do you think she'd date me? What does she like? How can I get her to fall in love with me? Tell me everything, Shark. Go."

Emilia slowly blinks at me and shakes her head, "You want her to fall in love with you? Really?"

I nod at her like one of those toy dogs my papa had in the back of his car when I was little.

"Yeah, I know, I've only met her once but I really like her. We talked over lunch. It took a bit of time for her to warm up to me, but when she did, something sparked. She's beautiful, intelligent, funny. Plus her name is Cleopatra and I'm Antony. It's like she was made for me, like we're destined to be together forever. I want to take her to see the play. I want to date her. Win her over with our namesakes. Have the forever kind of love with her that I've always wanted. The kind from the books."

She tilts her head to the side and stares at me, her eyes narrowing as she scrutinises my face.

"Fuck. You're serious!" she exclaims as she lowers her face to stare at her desk, but not before I notice the frown on her face. "Another one bites the dust. I'm going to be the last fucking Cooper sister standing." She brings her head up to look at me again, and instead of saying a word I listen. She studies me again and then with a hint of disbelief in her voice says, "The look in your eyes when you talk about her, it's the same as... Never mind." She sits forward in her chair, annoyance flashing through her catlike eyes at letting her facade slip, and rests her cheek on her hand.

"Poor little Cleopatra doesn't know what's about to come her way. The school of Cooper is in session, Antony. Pay attention. Cleo is a complicated little creature. She's the self-professed queen of darkness, but actually she isn't dark at all. She hates mornings—do not be all chirpy with her in the morning if you don't want to be throat punched. She's sarcastic as fuck and her sense of humour is dry, but she has the kindest heart and would bend over backwards to help someone she cares about. She's fiercely loyal and expects it back or she cuts you loose. Some call it cut-throat, I call it clever.

"I've never seen her in a relationship, so I can't give you any information on what she's like as a girlfriend, but I can tell you she's the best sister. She loves fiercely and makes me laugh like no other. Her family and friends mean more to her than anything, and if you're lucky enough to be welcomed into that circle, don't fuck it up.

"She loves drawing. She's really good at it but doesn't do it nearly enough anymore. She doodles sunflowers onto everything though. When she's on the phone she'll draw them subconsciously and when she sees one, they never fail to make her smile. They're her favourite flower, in case you couldn't tell." She pauses and sits forward again. She narrows her eyes and glares into mine. The glint in them causes perspiration to form on my upper lip and I can't help the gulp that follows from me.

"Antony, seriously, she's the best fucking person you'll ever meet. She deserves someone who will love her for who she is, someone that will cherish her. If you hurt her in any way, I *will* chop your balls off and wear them as earrings. Capiche, Marcello?

I gulp and nod my head. "Capiche, Cooper. I think I love her a little bit more after all of that."

Emilia stares at me wide eyed. "Love her? You just met her."

I scratch the back of my neck. "I know but…," I blow out a breath, "all jokes aside, I feel like she's perfect for me. I've always believed in love at first sight. My dad fell in love with my mum at first sight, and I fell for Cleopatra the minute I saw her. There's just something telling me she's mine. That she's meant for me." I look at Emilia and she nods her head at me.

She smiles as she tells me, "You just went up a million percent in my estimations, Antony. Good luck."

I exhale a loud breath and grin back at her. "Just think, if this goes well, I could be your future brother-in-law." I laugh as I watch the horror form on her face.

"Good god, what have I done? I take it all back. She's a nightmare. She smells and has a big, huge boyfriend who'll kick your arse, Marcello. Marcello?" I stand up and walk out of the office still laughing as I hear her calling me over and over again. She can protest all she wants but she secretly loves the idea of me being her brother-in-law. She just doesn't want to admit it.

CHAPTER 5

Ellipses are annoying and so is Emilia - Group texts

Emilia: Cleopatra…

Cleo: Emilliaaaaaaa…

Emilia: Had a meeting with your client today…

Nell: Why do you keep ending messages with ellipses? It's annoying!

Emilia: Nell, you're not the grammar police and we are not your students.

Nell: Jeez, you're mean today.

Cleo: Is there a point to these messages, Emilia? Some of us are trying to work. I'm not above throat punching you to get some quiet around here. Remember that, Sis.

Emilia: Oh there's a point, Cleopatra.

Emilia: Nell, that's the second time I've been called mean today. Actually, I was asked if meanness is a genetic thing that runs through the Cooper sisters' veins. Isn't that strange, Cleopatra? I wonder why someone would think us Cooper sisters are all mean? Hmmmmm (Thinking Emoji)

Cleo: Emilia. I'm going to phone you in a second. You better answer.

Emilia: Or what?

Cleo: I'll come to your office and throat punch you in front of everyone. ANSWER. THE. PHONE.

Nell: Why are you calling her? Emilia, what's going on?

Nell: Emilia? Cleo?

Juliet: What did I miss?

Nell: I couldn't tell you even if I wanted to, Princess.

CHAPTER 6

Fucking Emilia. She's been annoying me for days. It started off with the message in the sisters group chat and then carried on with our phone call when she finally answered. She, of course, gave me no information at all about what she and Twatface were talking about and neither would he when we had our 'working' dinner later that evening. I know they spoke about me, though. Nothing else could explain how he suddenly knew all about my love of sunflowers. He must've dropped them into our dinner conversation at least a dozen times. As well as the notebook he gave me. I let a brief smile cross my lips as I remember our dinner.

Nerves filter through my stomach as I enter the restaurant. I quickly shake them away, cracking my neck searching for my target while taking in the other diners as well. A couple at a nearby table give me a snide look and I roll my eyes whilst putting my hand on my hip, before fixing them with a pointed glare. They quickly focus on their plates and I smirk in victory. This may be a hoity toity restaurant but I'm done with feeling out of place. If I want to wear a tight black dress and yellow converse trainers to dinner, I will. My feet hurt and I refuse to wear heels when I'm having to get across town. I'm here for a business meeting. I deserve to be here and they can fuck right off if they don't like it.

The Maître'd escorts me to my table where Mr. Sunshine himself is already waiting. Those nerves I shook away hit me like a truck when my eyes lock with his, and I lose my breath at the intensity at which he's looking at me. I blink a few times and lower my head to hide my attraction. I take a few deep breaths and offer him my hand when I reach the table. Like a good businesswoman. He stands to greet me and I regret my footwear choice as he towers over me. With a blush across my cheeks, that I hate, I stand as tall as I can and wait. He doesn't take my hand at first. He watches me. His eyes burning into me fiercely. I start to squirm and I'm just about to bring my hand back when he smiles at me, mischief twinkling in his gaze, and finally takes my hand.

He doesn't shake it though. He lifts it to his mouth and brushes his lips over it, mumbling "Mia Regina." I have no fucking clue what his words mean but, my God, his lips on my skin make me want to drop my reservations and my knickers. I clear my throat and bring my hand back. I tuck my hair behind my ear and raise my eyebrow. "Still not being professional, Mr. Marcello?"

He grins, walking around to my chair to pull it out for me. I smirk as I sit down, thankful for the reprieve from his stare.

"I told you, I'm a professional on the pitch. Off it, I'm just a lovable idiot, Cleopatra." I don't flinch at his use of my name this time. My stupid body seems to like hearing my name on his lips.

"I got you something. To help with the planning." He winks, and again, I feel my cheeks start to heat. Annoyed with the way my body is showing him things I don't want him to know, I take a sip of my water.

"You really didn't need to. I have everything I need." I try to fill my voice with nonchalance but it comes out robotic. I *swear I'm going to the doctor's about this body and the way it's behaving.*

*"You may have all you **think** you need, Cleopatra. But sometimes we get something that we didn't **know** we needed, and it makes everything better."*

I bring my eyes up to look at him and find his gaze locked onto me. Flames flickering behind the whiskey colour of his eyes. He looks away and reaches under the table for something. As he slides the package wrapped in brown paper across the table at me I stare at it.

"It won't bite you, Cleopatra. Open it."

I shake my head, "No. You're my client, Mr. Marcello, you shouldn't be giving me gifts."

He rolls his eyes, huffing out a sigh. "I am your client but I'm also your friend. It's a notebook, to help with planning. Now will you open it?"

I let out an exasperated breath and tear open the paper. I move the tissue paper aside, and staring back at me is a beautiful notebook covered in bright yellow sunflowers. I look up at him with a scowl.

He laughs loudly. "You know most people say thank you, not scowl, but I know what you mean. You're welcome, Cleopatra."

I should have been annoyed that he went to my sister about me, but I found it endearing. He took the time to find out what I liked. It made me happy, I guess. I definitely think I need to book a doctor's appointment to see if there's something wrong with me as I'm not acting like the Cleo Cooper I've been all of my life.

Emilia must think this is hilarious. It's not. It's really fucking embarrassing. I have a crush on my client. I mean, I know a lot of women do as the man is unbelievable.

He's drop dead gorgeous.

Successful, charming, charismatic, intelligent and annoying all at the same time.

I'm insanely attracted to him but also acutely annoyed by him. And Emilia knows this. She's giving me sly looks and keeps smirking at me whenever she's around. It's infuriating. He's a client and a fucking footballer, to add insult to injury. I know what footballers are like. I've spent enough time with them to know they're all a bunch of untrustworthy dicks. I've seen the articles on his teammate Jaxson Brady, I know what they all get up to. Rich, arrogant, tossers who treat women like commodities and think they can do what the fuck they want because they have money, fame and power. I'm not being dragged into that circus with Marcello. No fucking way. I'll keep my crush on the down low and throat punch Emilia if she gets too much with the constant wind ups and jibes about 'being the last Cooper standing'.

The good thing about the constant messages and meetings with him? We've managed to lock down a number for the party and a few possible venues we're arranging to visit this week. The bad thing? It means more time spent with Twat-face—who I'm starting to realise isn't much of a twatface at all. But the name's kind of stuck with my family now. Only Emilia knows that Twatface is Antony Marcello the famous footballer, and it needs to stay that way. I can't have an events company that doesn't keep client information discreet.

I snuggle onto the sofa and rest my head on Juliet's lap when the ringtone for a video call interrupts the film we're watching. I reach over to the coffee table to grab the tablet and see Verity's name flash on my screen. I swipe the call open and smile when I see her beaming and very red looking face.

"Verity, did you forget to put on suncream? You're a redhead, you can't forget, EVER!" I laugh and tell her as Juliet giggles next to me.

Verity huffs her indignation at me, "I did not forget sunblock, Cleo. I take my skincare very seriously, you know that. We were on JP's yacht today and for some reason the sun affects me differently when I'm at sea. Anyway, how's work? How are you liking dealing with Antony?" I turn my startled eyes to her and she waves her hand at my worry. "Juliet can know his first name, she works for us. It's fine."

"I've only known him as Twatface so it's nice to know he has an actual name." Juliet pipes up and I wince as Verity's voice angrily scolds me.

"You call him Twatface? Cleopatra Cooper. How could you? He's the sweetest man on the planet and you call him Twatface. For shame on you." She tuts and folds her arms over her bikini clad breasts.

I can't help but giggle at the sight of her. "You know it's hard to take you seriously with a sunburnt face and your boobs squished together, looking like two angry bald men, don't you?" Juliet bursts into laughter and Verity cracks a smile too.

Jean-Pierre's thick, sexy French accent floats through the screen saying, "Zey are ze best looking bald men I've ever had ze privilege of getting to know, Bébé." I gag, Verity blushes, and Juliet sighs.

"Yuck, dude, not cool. Before he starts talking again, I'll fill you in on all of the details for the party but please, for the love of God, cover those bad boys up. Or JP might have to fight me for zem." I put on a French accent to mimic him and smile when I hear his chuckles. He even laughs in a French accent. I love him, even if he did steal my best friend away from me.

CHAPTER 7

As the weeks go by – Group texts

Antony/Twatface: Send me your address, I've seen something I want to send you.

Cleo: No.

Antony/Twatface: Come on. It's been two weeks since we met and I've spoken to and seen you everyday for most of that time. Surely you know I'm not a stalker by now.

Cleo: Read your message back and tell me that doesn't sound like the very definition of a stalker…

Antony/Twatface: What I class as friendship, you class as stalkerish. I'm an optimist and you're a pessimist. Opposites attract.

Cleo: (Laughing emoji face)

Antony/Twatface: A stalker wouldn't make you laugh. Just saying

Cleo: What did you want to send me?

Antony/Twatface: Tell me your address and I'll send it

Cleo: No.

Antony/Twatface: Okay. Send me a picture of you.

Cleo: More chance of the address…

Antony/Twatface: I'm playing away from home, lonely, sad and missing my friend. One picture?

Cleo: No

Antony/Twatface: How about a date? We can go and see a play?

Cleo: Night, Antony.

Antony/Twatface: It'll help with the party planning.

Cleo: How?

Antony/Twatface: It'll give me the chance to show you a bit of romance and once I do, Cleopatra, it will unlock that heart of yours and free you up to fall in love with a certain tall, dark and handsome person…

Cleo: Pass.

Antony/Twatface: For real?

Cleo: Night.

~

Antony/Twatface: What about a black and white theme for the party? Women in black, men in white?

Cleo: Blah

Antony/Twatface: Rude! Do you have any ideas? You keep vetoing mine.

Cleo: I have lots of ideas. This is my job after all. I just save mine for our actual meetings.

Antony/Twatface: You're mean but I kinda like it (winking emoji) Let's meet Wednesday for a lunch meeting?

Cleo: (Eyeroll emoji) Fine.

Cleo: How about fancy dress?

Antony/Twatface: For our lunch? I think it's a bit extra but I'm always up for extra, Cleopatra (winking emoji)

Cleo: I meant for the party. We can wear normal business attire for our lunch.

Antony/Twatface: Spoilsport

Cleo: I prefer the term "Professional." Anyway, back to the party. I know a guy that sorts out amazing costumes.

Antony/Twatface: Who?

Cleo: What does that matter? Fancy dress, yay or nay?

Antony/Twatface: Depends. Who's this guy you speak so highly of?

Cleo: Speak so highly of? I said I knew a guy. That was it. Why are you being weird?

Antony/Twatface: Well I've known you for over two weeks now and you've never mentioned another guy before.

Cleo: (Eyeroll emoji)

Antony/Twatface: I'm just kidding, kind of. But I want you to like me enough to agree to a date with me, so I'll be cool. What kind of fancy dress?

Cleo: You're a client, no dates. It should be themed. It's an engagement party so it has to be lovey dovey. That's where your brain comes into play…

Antony/Twatface: Erm… red hearts?

Cleo: Are you fucking serious? Red hearts? Mr. I-love-every-thing-about-love suggests red fucking hearts? I could've come up with that and my soul's black.

Antony/Twatface: There was too much pressure. I couldn't think on the spot. Give me a few days.

Antony/Twatface: And your soul isn't black. It's sunflower yellow. I've seen it through your eyes when you smile.

Cleo: I don't know how to respond to that.

Antony/Twatface: You don't have to.

Antony/Twatface: And FYI I'm a friend too. Not just a client. Admit it.

Antony/Twatface: What costumes has he sorted out for you before?

Cleo: An annoying friend, I'll admit that. We dressed up for my nephew's birthday which was superhero themed.

Antony/Twatface: But still a friend, my plan of wearing you down is working muhahaha.

Antony/Twatface: Who did you go as? I bet you looked sexy as hell dressed in a tight leather catsuit.

Cleo:...

Antony/Twatface: Sorry. Away games make me lonely. Staying in hotels, strange cities. I dunno (man shrugging emoji)

Cleo: I'm sure there are plenty of wannabe WAG's to keep you company. Don't hesitate on my part.

Antony/Twatface: Do I detect a hint of jealousy there?

Cleo: None, whatsoever. Might give me some peace if you fucked a WAG, to be fair.

Antony/Twatface: Yeah, there probably are a few I could find but I don't want them or that.

Cleo: What do you want then?

Antony/Twatface: I want the forever kind of love, not the fleeting one, with someone I was meant to be with.

Cleo: Erm... so fancy dress then?

Antony/Twatface: Avoidance tells me more than you know, Cleopatra. Goodnight.

~

Antony/Twatface: Dinner tonight?

Antony/Twatface: A 'working' dinner, of course (winking emoji)

Antony/Twatface: Cleopatra?

Antony/Twatface: Why are you ignoring me?

Cleo: I'm not ignoring you. I just want to be left alone today, Antony.

Antony/Twatface: Why?

Antony/Twatface: Is something wrong?

Antony/Twatface: Let me help.

Antony/Twatface: Come on Cleo. I've known you now for over three weeks. We talk daily, sometimes multiple times, and we've been out together nearly every day doing 'work' things. I can help. Tell me what's wrong. Please.

Cleo: God, you're infuriating. All I wanted was to be left alone on my Saturday off, but no, you won't have it. I swear men never fucking listen. Fine, you want to know. I came on my fucking period and I'm cramping like a bitch and I just want to be left alone today.

Antony/Twatface: Send me your address please. I promise I won't come over.

Cleo: No.

CHAPTER 8

My stomach is killing me, my head hurts and I can't find a fucking hot water bottle. All I want to do is curl into a ball with some heat on my belly and scoff some calorie filled goodies whilst reading a book before I have to go fucking bowling with everyone tonight to help Connor with Juliet. But I can't. Juliet's eaten all of the chocolate. The joys of living with another woman and having your cycles sync up means they take your period supplies and don't replace them in time for you to use them.

My phone beeps with another text message but I ignore it. I can't deal with Antony. I don't want to snap or be horrible to him, and with the way I'm feeling, I know I will. Instead of looking at it, I run a bath and hope the painkillers kick in enough for me to hunt my bloody hot water bottle down.

The painkillers are working their magic but I couldn't find the hot water bottle. I still don't have any chocolate either, but it's a small price to pay for an empty apartment and a non-buzzing phone. It's been two hours since my last text to

Antony and I think I may have finally managed to push him away. I didn't mean to be so harsh with him, but he was irritating me. And I really don't want him to have my address. It's too personal. He needs to remain as much of a client as I can maintain. I know I'm not doing a great job with all the texting, the flirty banter, and seeing him everyday that I can, but the address thing I can put a stop to.

"Delivery for Cleopatra Cooper. Answer the door." I roll my eyes at Emilia's voice and stomp over to the front door. I swing it open and come face to face with a smug look and a hamper she's holding in her hands.

"What the fuck is that and what do you want? I'm dealing with the mother of all periods, Em."

She grimaces in sympathy. "I come bearing gifts. A certain someone messaged me and asked for your address. Obviously if he was asking me, it meant you hadn't given it to him, so I gave him mine. He knows it's mine, but he also knows I will skin him alive if he dares to turn up or tell any of my other clients where I live, so it's fine. I trust him. This is for you." She hands over the hamper, turns on her heel, and walks a few spaces away before turning back to me.

"He's a good guy, Cleo. Jokes aside, he really likes you. What harm is there in giving him a chance? I don't know what your damage is, you won't tell me, but I know a genuine guy when I see one and he's as genuine as they come. And he's a footballer, have you seen those thighs?"

She bites down on her lip and presses the lift button. The doors open immediately for her and I chuckle at the notion of anything defying Emilia as I close the door. I place the hamper on the coffee table and open up the note.

I listen to you, even when you're silent, I'm listening. I'll always give you what you ask for even when you don't say the words. I hope these help. Goodnight, Cleopatra. Yours, Antony XxX

A tear trickles down my cheek and I swipe it away. Stupid hormones. This guy can't be for real. The last guy that worked this hard to get me to like him turned out to be a cheating scumbag who humiliated me. I'm not built for this kind of love. I'm mean, sarcastic, and I prioritise everything before a boyfriend. I shake my head to rid myself of the hormone induced emotion and open up the hamper.

Laughter bubbles up inside of me when I spot fluffy sunflower socks and dark grey fluffy pjs. An abundance of chocolate fills the hamper, along with a hot water bottle, bath bombs and face masks. It's the ultimate period supply hamper. How did he manage to source all of this so quickly?

"Duh, Cleo. He's a multimillionaire, professional foot-baller. He tells people to jump and they say how high," I tell myself as I reach for my phone. I bring our text conversation up and see the unread text message I ignored earlier.

Twatface: Don't be mad at me. I messaged Emilia. I care about you, Cleopatra and I don't like the idea of you being in pain and alone. I'm sorry if it went too far out of the 'friend/client' zone x

Another tear trickles down my cheek and I slump onto the sofa. This is why I don't do emotions. This is why I have sex with friendly boys and not boyfriends. I don't understand all of this. Is he genuine? How can I tell without risking myself again? I don't want to be embarrassed in front of all of my family this time, but I also don't want to not respond to him.

My body, my emotions, and my heart are all telling me to dive in head first with Antony—to make some happy memories to replace the old—but my head is reminding me of the betrayal, hurt, and humiliation I felt the last time I did that. The whole campus knew he fucked my flatmate, but I managed to keep it from my sisters. I wouldn't be so lucky the second time around. And definitely not this close to home.

I wish I could talk to them. Juliet has her own stuff going on with Connor. Nell is all loved up and in nesting family mode, so happy with Will and patiently waiting for my niece to be born. Emilia just told me her two pennies worth. So that leaves Marcus and Verity, and I don't want to discuss this with either of them. Plus, besides Verity, no one else knows about Alex the fucktwat from uni.

I snap a picture of the inside of the hamper and write out a text to Antony. I have to apologise and I want to thank him, but I hesitate before sending it.

Me: Thank you. This is very sweet, Antony. I'm sorry I snapped at you over text. I like that you listen, even when I'm silent x

Should I put the x at the end? Is that message taking it a step too far? What do I want from all of this?

I groan in frustration at my own stupid thoughts and throw my phone down on the sofa. The little whooshing sound rings out in the silence of my living room letting me know my message has been sent and brings me out of my pity party. Panic grips me as I grab my phone from the sofa.

"Shit! I didn't want to send that. Great and he's fucking responding." I curse at myself.

I anxiously chew on my bottom lip waiting for his reply and jump when my phone vibrates and beeps in my hand.

Twatface: Don't worry about it. I grew up with lots of female cousins so I know what it's like. Women are amazing. So much stronger than men. My mama's the strongest woman in the world. She managed me and my papa—who is exactly like me BTW—on a day to day basis and didn't murder us.

She also kicked cancer's arse a year ago. Strongest woman ever x

I breathe a sigh of relief, he skipped past the listening part, thank God.

Me: We are strong. We're built that way. You're telling me there are two of you? Jeez x
Me: I'm sorry your mum had to go through that but I'm happy she kicked its fucking arse x
Twatface: Lol. Don't swear, Cleopatra x
Me: Fuck off, you're not my mum x
Twatface: (Man shrugging emoji) erm obviously… x
Me: (Eyeroll emoji) She's the only one I don't swear in front of x
Twatface: Ah noted. If you ever meet my mama, don't swear in front of her either. She'll think nothing of cuffing you around the ear lol x
Me: Noted. I doubt I'll meet her though. Unless she's coming to the party? x
Twatface: No, she isn't. You will one day though. I know it. Come out with me tomorrow? x
Me: I don't think so. We're having a family Sunday dinner at my sister's x
Twatface: Can I come? x
Me: No, Antony x
Twatface: Sorry. You've told me so much about them that I feel like I know them. I forget I haven't met them yet. x

This guy is too much. Everything he says sounds perfect. Would it hurt to go out with him? My head screams, '*Yes, it would hurt,*' as my heart screams, '*No, go for it. We deserve this.*'

Me: If it's for work, I can cancel and be free though x

What am I doing? Do I really want to go out with him tomorrow? Yes, yes I do. Even if it's under the guise of work, I really want to spend time with him.

Twatface: It's totally for work. I have tickets to a play so we can see the venue. It could work for the party x

I laugh as I read his text, knowing full well we aren't going to check out the venue and that he just wants to take me out.

Me: What time tomorrow? x
Twatface: Two pm x
Me: Pick me up? x
Twatface: Funny. I don't have your address x
Me: Actually you do, well part of it anyway. I live in the same building as Emilia. I'll meet you outside at two. Thank you, Antony x
Twatface: My pleasure, Cleopatra x

CHAPTER 9

Antony

I button up my black shirt and roll the sleeves up to my forearms before grabbing the biker boots from my wardrobe and shoving my feet into them. I've opted for an all black look today to match my Queen of Darkness, but I've also included a little yellow sunflower pin which my amazing assistant sourced for me yesterday whilst she was getting the hamper sorted. I know it's cheesy, and a little bit silly, but hopefully it'll make Cleopatra smile.

Cleopatra. It's been over a month since we first met and we've spent nearly every one of those days together in one form or another. We've spoken over text every day and I feel like I really know her. She acts all snarky but she's shown her softer side to me. When she talks about her family, the love shines off her. She's rooting for her sister, Juliet, and her best friend, Connor, to finally get together. Where some would've been jealous that her sister and bestie were hooking up, she's happy for them. Even going so far as to help him win her over. She pretends seeing her oldest sister Nell in love and happy with her partner Will makes her heave, but the smile that takes over her whole face when she thinks of them is another story altogether. Without even meaning to, she's opened up to me.

She doesn't wait for me to text first and she messages me as much as I do her. I know she likes me, she wouldn't be wasting her time with me if she didn't. Yes, she has to bother with me for work, but if there were no feelings there she'd send emails and on a need-to-know-basis only. She wouldn't have told me anything personal about herself either. Plus, Emilia told me she does. I didn't mean to discuss her with Shark, but when Cleo wouldn't give me her address, I had no choice but to ask her sister. Was it a bit stalkerish of me? Yes. Would I do it again? Yes, yes I would. I needed Cleo to know that she could depend on me, even if it's just as a friend.

Emilia told me not to give up, and once she'd delivered the hamper to her, she texted to tell me I'd done the right thing. In Shark's language, that's basically a seal of approval.

I jump into my car and head over to her building. Nerves are bubbling in my stomach like what I'd get before a big match. I take a deep breath and blow it out slowly. I do this over and over again until the nerves subside and I'm left roaring to go. I know I've spent time with her before, but this time feels different. It feels like we're going on a real date. Something about her texts was different and I'm optimistic that we're taking the next step in our friendlationship.

Hopefully it won't be the only date we get to go on. I want to win this woman over. I want her to fall so in love with me that she can't go a minute without texting, touching, or thinking about me. Like I am with her. She's already doing the texting. Which makes me believe she's also already doing the thinking. And the only thing that's stopping me from touching her all the time is that I know she isn't ready yet. But I'm hoping we're a step closer, and will be even closer again after today.

I smile as I pull up to her building and watch her roll her eyes at me from the pavement. She holds her hand up at me, halting my movements as I go to get out, then she opens the door, jumps into the passenger seat and punches me in the arm, hard.

"Ow, Cleopatra. What was that for?"

She turns in her seat to face me as I rub my arm and frown at her. "That was for telling Emilia that you were taking me out on a date to see 'Antony and Cleopatra' because we are destined to be together because of our names. She then told Nell, who thought it was hilarious to tell my mum, who now thinks we're going to get married, have babies and live in the countryside somewhere. Ugh. Never tell Emilia anything, Antony."

I open my mouth to say something but can't because what she just described is everything I want. But if I tell her that she'll think I'm crazy. So instead I just grin at the little fantasy in my head as she reaches over her shoulder and puts her seatbelt on. I take a second to let my eyes roam over her body. She looks fucking amazing. A tight black dress hugs every curve she has, and I am here for her curves. Her hair is down, framing her beautiful face. It's so shiny and looks so soft that I want to reach out and stroke it. I don't because my arm still hurts from the punch she gave me and I don't want another one for touching her without permission. She's done something different with her make up today too. Her eyes look bigger and, for some reason, more vulnerable. I can't stop looking at her. She's breathtaking. She catches me and I grin at her.

"You look good, Cleopatra. I forgive you for hitting me by the way."

Her nostrils flare as she keeps in her laughter and shakes her head at me whilst trying to hide her smile. "You forgive me? I just had to endure a ten minute phone call from my mum. She kept asking when I was going to tell her I'd met the love of my life. I think she's just mad that you're named after a Shakespearean character and she didn't know, to be fair."

As I pull away from her building, I chuckle and ask her, "Well, when were you going to tell her? She should have been the first person you told, my little sunflower. She is your mother after all. She shouldn't have to hear it from your sisters."

She turns to face me as much as the seatbelt will allow, crossing her legs toward me and I fight to keep my eyes on the road.

"Don't make me throat punch you when you're driving, Antony. Why did you tell Emilia anyway?"

I shrug my shoulders, "I didn't think it was a big deal."

She rolls her eyes at me and shakes her head. "You don't have siblings, I keep forgetting. Emilia and I love each other dearly, but we also love to wind each other up. She got the ultimate leverage over me, courtesy of you."

I grin over at her and wink, "Sorry, Sunflower."

She blows out a breath and mumbles, "You're seriously sticking with Sunflower? I think I preferred Cleopatra better."

I can't fight the laughter that spills out of my mouth. I catch the grin that plants itself firmly on her face when she makes me laugh and it sends little flutters through my chest. "Anyway, what's wrong with being married to me, having babies, and living in the countryside? I think we'd have beautiful babies." I watch her out of the corner of my eye and note that her body stiffens a little but I see the flicker of a smile on her mouth before she schools her features back into a non-fussed look.

"That's a given, we're both hot as fuck. Our babies would

be beautiful by default. Getting married is bad enough, but living in the country, no thank you. I'm never moving out of the city. London is my bitch." She laughs as she talks and I can't help but grin along with her.

"So you think I'm hot as fuck. Good to know, Cleopatra. I have to disagree though. I think it's better if we raise our kids out of the city. What if we compromise and move to Hertfordshire? You said your parents live there. And Nell. Our kids could go to school with their cousins." I wait expectantly, but also a bit apprehensively, hoping she doesn't clam up and plays along with my little fantasy.

She scrunches her face up in thought and looks absolutely adorable. I won't tell her that though as I'm sure I'd get another punch to the arm for it. She pouts her lips as she ponders my question and I want to kiss her so much. To taste her and smudge that red lipstick painted on her perfect lips. I won't though. Not until she tells me it's okay.

"Alright, the kids being close to each other is a must but that can still happen with us in London. I couldn't live that close to my mum and Nell, they'd drive me mad…"

She stops talking and I can pinpoint the very moment she realises what's been coming out of her mouth. Nervously shifting in her chair, she bites on her bottom lip. "Why are we even talking about this? We aren't fucking dating, let alone having kids together. Jeez." A pink hue faintly covers her cheeks and I grin at her, knowing she's embarrassed at how open she just was.

"If you say so, Sunflower." I smile at her and wink again and the pink turns to a full-on red. I have to touch her, reassure her that it's okay, so I reach over and take her hand. I bring it to my mouth and kiss the back of it. She averts her eyes from me but doesn't snatch it back when I rest our hands together on the console between our seats, and we drive the rest of the way to the theatre, silently holding hands.

~

"Man, I forgot how much I love Shakespeare. Even after all of these years his words are so poignant. He really is the greatest writer of all time, isn't he?" She smiles at me as we sit at the private bar I'm a member of that's around the corner from the theatre.

I shrug. "I don't know, I kind of can't understand a lot of his words. Thee, thou and all of that, it's confusing."

Her mouth drops open and her eyes are as wide as saucers as I take a sip of my water. "Did you only bring me to this play because of the title? You don't actually like Shakespeare?" She asks, her voice a couple of octaves higher than normal.

I chuckle and spin on my barstool so that I'm facing her directly and bring my gaze to focus on hers. Her pupils dilate, her breathing increases and I take a couple of seconds to just look at her.

"It was written thousands of years ago about two people who fell in love at first sight, even though they weren't supposed to. Who went against the odds and fought to be together. Two people with the same names as us. It felt apt." I reach over and take her hand again and lace our fingers together.

She breaks our gaze and stares down at our joined hands.

"Antony, what are you doing?" She groans out and I see her clench her thighs together, her desire for me as clear as the bulge pressing against the zipper of my jeans.

She wants me as badly as I want her, but that's not going to happen yet. She needs to be sure before I do anything to stop the ache in her pussy, even though it's all I want to do right now.

I shrug my shoulders at her and look into her eyes again.

"I'm just holding your hand, Sunflower. I like holding you, touching you. You make me feel, Cleopatra."

"Antony. I can't give you the forever kind of love you're looking for. I'm not built for that." She looks away when she says the last part, pain flashing across her face.

I squeeze her hand and she brings her eyes back to mine.

"I call bullshit, Cleopatra. Why do you say that?" My heart is racing in my chest, and I want—no, I need—her to tell me why she thinks she isn't capable of a forever kind of love. She's more than capable. She was built to love and love fiercely. I see it every time she speaks of her family. The way she took Connor under her wing at school and has loved him like a brother tells me that. The way her eyes light up when she talks about her nephew Ben and how excited she gets when she mentions her niece being born. She loves and she loves hard. I have no doubt her love is the forever kind. She's more than capable and was definitely built for an everlasting, epic kind of love. Instead of telling her this, I listen to what she has to say.

"I haven't told anyone this, Antony. Not my sisters or Connor, no one." She looks at me pointedly and I pretend to zip my lips closed and cross my heart with my hand. She smirks at me and carries on.

"I tried it once. In uni. Dating. A fucktwat called Alex pursued me. Chased me. Made promises to me. And against my better judgement, I believed him. We dated for seven months and what I thought was a sweet, happy relationship turned out to be a lie. I caught him fucking my flatmate on the bed we slept in together. He was a 'footballer' too." She pauses, straightens her shoulders, and reaches for her wine.

I give her a second to compose herself before I speak, and when she places the glass back down I tell her, "I'm sorry that dickhead broke your heart, Cleo…"

She spins her face toward mine furiously. "He didn't

break my heart. I didn't give it to him in the first place, so don't feel sorry for me, Antony. It was better like that anyway. He showed me I wasn't built for the 'norm.' Seven months I spent with him and I didn't really love him. I don't even think I really liked him. I just wanted to do what 'normal' people were doing. When I got to uni and saw people pairing off, I thought I *should try* to be 'normal.' Turns out I suck at being 'normal.'" She darts her gaze away from mine, but I can see the frown forming on her face before she shakes her head, sits straighter and brings her beautiful brown eyes back to mine.

I grin at her. "Normal's overrated. I prefer odd." I wink and she smiles whilst rolling her eyes.

She blows out a breath, "Apparently it was all my fault anyway. I didn't show him enough attention, studied too much and didn't support him enough. He could see I wasn't built for relationships, said I was more like a bloke—all about the fun times. I was pissed off and humiliated by him, but not broken-hearted. It did hurt when he said I was mean and looked like a kid, but I got over that pretty quickly. Everyone talking about us and feeling sorry for me annoyed me more than his words ever could."

It's my turn to interrupt. Anger shoots through me and I can't sit and listen anymore. I get off my chair and lean over her, my hands placed on either side of her body, caging her in as I ask, "He said what? You look like a...? No. I can't even... I'm going to need his full fucking name, Cleopatra. I'll be able to find him from that."

Irrational rage is seeping out of me. I know I should try to control it, but I can't. She's fucking perfect and some fucking idiot told her she wasn't. I can't let that slide. My breath is coming thick and fast and I frown down at her. Our gazes lock. Anger burning in my eyes and lust blazing in hers.

She reaches up and grabs the front of my shirt, and when

she gives it the slightest tug, I drop closer to her face. I feel her free hand wrap around my neck as she whispers, "You're really fucking hot when you're angry." She pulls my head down to her, and as our lips meet, heat shoots through my body.

It feels like my entire being is set alight. Every inch of me is ablaze in a fire of glory as her lips are finally mine. Sparks race from my mouth down to my dick and I groan as she bites my bottom lip. My hand snakes up and into her hair and I tug it a little to place her head where I want it. She moans into my mouth and I take the opportunity to slide my tongue against hers and relish in her taste. When she slides her fingers into my hair, I press my lips to hers harder, wanting to bruise her mouth so everyone will know she's mine. She's filling all of my senses. Her smell, her taste, her sounds, they all engulf me and I'm lost to my Cleopatra. Another moan brings me back to my senses and with a behemoth amount of strength, I break away from her, pleased to hear her disappointed little gasp.

Dazed, she brings her hand to her lips and runs her thumb over them then whispers, "Eternity was in our lips and eyes. Dammit, Antony."

I sit back in my chair, still holding her hand as confusion swims through me. She must see it as she tells me, "It was a quote from the play."

"I don't remember hearing 'dammit, Antony' in the play." I smile at her to try to take some of the worry away from her face but she just frowns at me.

"That part was a Cleo original, said because you made me quote Shakespeare. No one has done that before." She wriggles her fingers that are still entwined with my own and slides her hand from my grasp.

"Talk to me, Cleopatra. You didn't like our kiss?" I ask,

trying to pull her from her own head and bring her back into our space.

"I did. And that's the problem. I liked it more than I've ever liked anything, Antony. It made me want more. And wanting more isn't something I know how to do. Being vulnerable and open for hurt isn't something I think I can manage. I've never wanted the norm; marriage, kids, happily ever afters. But you make me question what I thought I knew I wanted. I don't do feelings and emotions and you, Antony, are all about feelings and emotions."

She dips her head down so her chin is on her chest and I reach over to her. I cup her chin gently with my hand and bring her head back up. I lean over her a little so our faces are inches away. "Who said we have to be one thing and one thing only, Cleopatra? You can still be the Queen of Darkness whilst being happy. You don't have to label this and rush out to buy a wedding dress or anything. We can just be Cleopatra and Antony. Queen of Darkness and Mr. Sunshine. You can be my Sunflower, while still being a bad arse boss lady. Opposites attract, Cleo. You don't have to be emotional and all about the feelings, I've got you covered there. But don't run away from your feelings either. Please."

She nods her head gently and I run my thumb over her bottom lip. "Come on, I'll take you home. You've got work in the morning, Sunflower."

I grab her hand and she remains silent as we walk out to the car park. She still hasn't said anything as we drive home. I pull up outside her building, switch the engine off, and turn in my seat.

"Goodnight, Sunflower."

She opens her mouth to speak but closes it again without saying anything. Instead, she nods at me and reaches her hand over the middle console, lacing her fingers over the top of mine and staring at our joined hands. She squeezes tightly and lets go, opens the car door and jumps out as quickly as her high heels will carry her. I watch her go into her building before driving away feeling optimistic, happy, and scared all at the same time. She's right, I'm all about the fucking feelings.

CHAPTER 10

Cleo

I stumble through my door and I'm assaulted by a flying couch cushion. Looking in the direction the projectile came from, I see Princess sitting on the sofa. Waiting for me. Because of course she is. I throw off the torture devices I've been wearing on my feet for the past few hours and try to avoid my sister's questions about why I'm dressed for a date when I was supposed to be seeing a play for work with Twat-face. Sometimes being close to your siblings is a pain in the arse.

She's grilling me, but I can see on her face she's just deflecting something that's bothering her. I really don't want to dissect her issues with Connor again, not tonight—and not when I have my own issues with a man—but she's my little sister and clearly needs my help. Connor's my brother from another mother; if I can do anything to help them finally realise they're perfect for each other, I will. My issues can wait, but Juliet's obviously can't if she's launching the soft furnishings about. I sigh and head into the kitchen whilst telling Juliet, "This sounds like it's going to be a long conversation so I'm grabbing some wine and getting comfortable, chick."

Once I've finally managed to convince Juliet to stop overthinking and just go for it with Connor, I head to my bedroom and flop onto my bed. Images of Antony fly through my mind and I groan and pull the pillow over my face. What is wrong with me? Why am I making such a big deal about this? I like him, he likes me. Why can't I just go with the flow?

Because he doesn't deserve to be hurt.

The words I just uttered to Juliet about Connor slap me in the face. I don't want to hurt him. He deserves to have that forever kind of love he told me he wants. I just don't think I can give it to him. I wasn't lying earlier when I said Alex the fucktwat didn't break my heart. He didn't, but he taught me a valuable lesson. I'm not built for relationships.

If I were to date Antony, the same patterns that happened with fucktwat would start to emerge. I'd get busy at work, have less time for him, become more distant and mean, and he'd start to look elsewhere for affection and attention. The only difference is I don't know if I could cope with Antony doing that to me. I didn't really care about Alex, but Antony? Him, I care about a lot. I value the friendship we've built since that first lunch meeting and I don't want to lose that. He may be a twatface but he's *my* twatface.

I never thought I wanted to be in love. Never thought I'd want a guy to answer to. But after spending time with Antony, I like knowing there's someone who cares about me who's not related to, or dating someone who's related to me. Marcus is included in that as he's basically Emilia's gay husband.

Don't let the past make you scared of the future.

Again my own words from my talk with Juliet come back to bite me on the arse. Just because I thought it wasn't what I wanted doesn't mean it isn't what I want now. Just because it didn't work with Fucktwat doesn't mean it won't work with Antony. Nell and Will flash before my eyes, the happiness they have, the things they've had to overcome. A yearning deep inside of me stirs and I realise I want that. But it's more than that. I don't just want that with anyone, I want that with Antony. He's right, I'm growing to love his brand of oddness.

CHAPTER 11
Antony

I can't stop thinking about our kiss. I went home last night and headed straight to the shower to relieve some tension, but if anything it just made it worse. Fucking my hand is not what I want to be doing after sharing a kiss like that with Cleopatra. I want to be plunging inside of her and feeling her pussy cling to my dick, not wrapping my hand around it and jacking off. But that has to wait. I still have a lot to do to win her heart. I feel like we had a breakthrough last night. She enjoyed our date. She loved the play, and hopefully some of the love the actors portrayed for each other rubbed off on her.

She did kiss me. But she also retreated. I need to see her again. I want to keep the momentum up with her. I decided this morning I'd head over to her office after training. I want her to know that I'm all she needs and *she* is all that I want, exactly as she is. It pissed me off knowing she believed what her ex had to say about her—so much so I want to annihilate him. But I'll have the last laugh in the end when she and I are living our happily ever after together.

I pull up outside her office and check myself in the rearview mirror. She isn't expecting me but I'm hoping, after last night, she'll be happy to see me. I hop out of my car and check around for paparazzi, relieved when I see none. The fuckers are quite good about leaving us alone generally. The odd pap picture of us leaving a restaurant or something like that will appear every now and then. They go after the younger and inexperienced players more, the ones who aren't used to being rich and famous. The ones like Brady. He's been in the papers for all of the wrong reasons recently.

I run my hand through my hair, fix the collar of the dark blue shirt I'm wearing, and straighten the sunflower pin I'm still proudly sporting. I enter the building quietly and I'm shocked to see Cleopatra shouting at Juliet and Connor. I know it's them because she's shown me pictures of her whole family. I'm obviously walking into the tailend of their argument as Cleopatra very firmly tells them I'm a twatface who she isn't dating and isn't ever dating.

Hurt cascades through my body at the venom dripping from her words. I thought last night meant something to her. I was obviously mistaken.

I clear my throat and utter a reluctant, "Erm hi. I'm Antony Marcello, also known as Twatface apparently, the person she won't date and isn't dating ever. Nice to meet you. You must be Connor and Juliet. I've heard a lot about you. Shame your name isn't Romeo."

I grin at Connor who's staring at me slack-jawed—he clearly knows who I am. He shakes my hand and tells me he's a big fan and I nod and smile politely at him. My gaze is fixed on Cleopatra who looks at me with eyes as wide as saucers. The red tint on her face leads me to the assumption she's ashamed or angry—probably both.

My heart pounds as a need to comfort her ricochets through me. I want to make her forget about everything except how she felt in my arms, with our lips pressed together, but I won't. She very clearly stated she wasn't dating me and isn't interested in me. Consent is everything and I won't force her to do anything she doesn't want too. It has to be on her terms. And her terms were just screamed loud and clear.

I watch as nerves consume her normally cool demeanour and her teeth dig into her lip punishingly. Her eyes are pleading with me, willing me not to say anything in front of her family. Connor and her sister turn back to face her, and I watch the shutters come down on her emotive eyes, her features schooling into her Queen of Darkness look.

"Antony, why are you here?" She asks me. Her voice is cold and businesslike. Gone are the whispers of me being hot and her moans of pleasure.

I smile sadly at her, letting her see the pain of her words. "Antony and not Twatface now?"

She shrinks back a bit, guilt flashing through her eyes, quickly replaced by that pleading look again. I clear my throat and change the subject for her sake because even though she's hurt me, I still want to protect and look after this woman with every fibre of my being.

"I needed to speak to you about the theme. Zoe doesn't like it now. She said it's cliché. I tried calling you but it wouldn't connect so I thought I'd drop by." It's the only lie I can think of that sounds plausible. I'm not the greatest of liars so I had to keep it simple.

Her thankful eyes tell me all I need to know but I can't help but tell her, "Didn't think I'd walk in and hear you declaring your undying dislike for me." I shake my head, turn on my heel and shout back, "Call me when you have the time."

I storm out of the office and jump straight into my car and drive off. I know she isn't coming after me. I know she's got to process what just happened. What I don't know is if she *will* come after me at all.

As soon as I get home I head inside and fire up the computer so I can call the one person that will understand everything and make me see things clearly. My papa. I wasn't kidding when I said he's exactly like me. He thinks the same way I do and if anyone can help me make sense of this thing I have going on with Cleopatra it's him.

The video call connects and I laugh as I see my papa's eye pressed up to the screen.

"Papa, move your eye away from the camera." I chuckle, knowing he's just messing with me, pretending to be an old man who knows nothing of technology when in reality it's the opposite. I roll my eyes when he sits back and grins the same grin I have back at me.

"*Mio figlio*, how are you? It's been a while."

I know when he starts with *my son* before he raises an eyebrow, he's doing his version of scolding me. Papa was never one for discipline growing up—my mama was the bad cop to his good cop routine—but he's right, it has been a long time since I went over to see them. They live in Stresa, Italy and I used to visit all the time, but everything has gotten so busy with football, endorsements, and social engagements I haven't been able to get over there. Mama and Papa haven't been able to visit me either so we haven't seen each other in the flesh for a long time.

"Sorry Papa, I've been busy. It's no excuse, I know, but life gets in the way."

He nods his head at me and sits back in his chair, studying me, eyes narrowed, before he smirks and says, "Tell me about her, son."

I sigh, my papa knows me too well. "She's perfect. She's moody, sarcastic, beautiful, funny, has her own business, and doesn't want me. I hired her company to arrange Charlie and Zoe's engagement party. I think I fell in love the first time I saw her and that was before I even knew her name. We've been texting and seeing each other for over a month now under the guise of work related meetings, but last night we shared an unbelievable kiss and she still doesn't want me." I put my head in my hands and scrub at my face, feeling better for putting it all out there, but worse for hearing it all spoken as truth.

My papa leans closer to the screen. "She sounds like your mama before I tamed her. What's her name?"

His eyes are twinkling. He already knows but I tell him anyway.

"Cleopatra. And you really think you've tamed Mama?" I say with a smirk of my own, as I know what his reaction will be.

"*Grazie Dio*. You found her." He slaps his forehead as he *thanks God*. "Of course she doesn't want you. Have you even read about Cleopatra? She's strong, independent, feisty. She runs her own country *per l'amor di Dio*. She doesn't want to want Antony, but she does. Your Cleopatra will be conflicted if she's anything like your mama, you have to let her come to you." He smiles and shakes his head, muttering, "*For the love of God,*" but this time in English. He stands up, stretches and sits back down again, this time even closer to the screen so I can see the faint lines around his eyes and the grey in his dark hair. At sixty-two my papa looks incredible for his age and he knows it too.

With a grin on his face he whispers, "Son, these Cleopatras, they need to make the decisions, it's the way they're programmed. But it's our job to guide them and help them see that *we* are the right decision for *them*. Do you understand?"

He smiles and I know he's thinking of my mama and I grin back at him. Even after all this time, he loves her with a passion that I'm finally beginning to truly understand.

"I do, Papa. But I walked into her office to her calling me Twatface and telling her sister she's never going to date me.

She was pretty clear she doesn't want me. I need to respect that."

He guffaws at me. Actually guffaws. I don't think I've ever seen or heard anyone do that before.

"Your mother told my whole family she wouldn't be seen dead with me and later that night told me she loved me. You can't give up. She's expecting you to do that. She thinks if she pushes you away enough you'll take the option from her. She won't have to decide if she wants you or not. Let her know there is no option. Show her you're in it for the long haul. If you are, that is?"

He raises an eyebrow again and my eyes roll in my head. They've rolled so much during this conversation, I've given myself a headache.

"Of course I am, Papa. I just told you I fell in love almost instantly. Do you really think I'm not in it for the long haul? What should I do now then Mr. I-know-everything-there-is-to-know-about-Cleopatras?"

His laughter peels out from the screen and is loud enough to attract my mama's attention. She saunters over to stand behind him without him realising.

"Of course I know everything about Cleopatras…"

He doesn't get the chance to finish his sentence as my mama slaps him around the back of the head.

"You should only know and care about one Cleopatra, Mr. Marcello."

She gives him a fierce look.

He flings his arms wide open and declares through his smile, "There is and only ever has been one Cleopatra for this Antony, *Mia Regina. My Queen.*"

When he smiles up at her, her sternness fades from her face and she sits on his lap. She presses her lips to his cheek and he beams with happiness. He looks contentedly into the screen and winks at me as she rolls her eyes at the same time.

I shake my head at both of them as a pang of yearning strikes me in my chest. I want that with my Cleopatra. I want the banter, the bickering, the love. I want the easiness of it all. The comfortable, carefree love that lasts a lifetime because you just know how that other person ticks.

"Hey Mama, how are you?" My voice comes out raspy and thick with emotion.

"What's the matter? Are you okay?" The instant concern rings out in my mama's voice.

Papa gently rubs her back and tells her, "Patti, he's fine, Baby. He's having woman trouble with a girl called Cleopatra."

Papa's eyes twinkle as Mama slowly blinks at me. She leans closer to the screen and exclaims, "I'm going to need a hat for the wedding. I'll be mother of the groom. I'm so happy. But why did you tell him before me, huh?"

"What're you pouting about now, Bruh?" Brady asks as he comes into the gym, his water bottle in hand and his earbuds already in his ears. I'm standing on the treadmill, stationary, trying to figure out a brilliant theme I can text Cleopatra about.

I haven't heard from her since I walked out of her office yesterday. I've been tempted to text her some random crap to get a conversation going, but something's holding me back. If I can come up with a theme, it would give me a real work reason to contact her, and then she can apologise. I know she will. She just doesn't want to be the one to reach out first.

She's stubborn, but I love that. Being a famous footballer means you get a lot of allowances. Girls come on to you, people are always nice to you, you get free things given to you so you can promote them to your millions of followers on the gram or TikTok. It's nice having to work for something for a change. I like that I have to chase her, woo her a little.

"Nothing. I'm concentrating, not pouting, you douche." I throw back at Brady.

He laughs and shakes his head, "I should never have told you that word. Still can't believe ya'll don't use that over here. And that's not your concentration face, that's your pouting face, Marcello. What's up?" He folds his arms over his chest and raises his eyebrows at me.

I try to glare back at him but instead grin mischievously as a thought enters my mind. "Okay, if I tell you what's wrong with me, you have to tell me what was going on with that pretty little redhead you were arguing with the other day."

I watch as his eyes darken when I call her pretty and a frown forms on his already glaring face. "Forget it," he tells me and turns to step onto the treadmill next to me. He fiddles with his phone and I can hear music blaring from his earbuds.

Guilt washes over me. This kid's obviously going through something and I shouldn't be winding him up. I tap his shoulder and he sighs and takes the buds out of his ears. "Brady, I'm sorry. If you want to talk about it though, for real, all jokes aside, I'm here."

He blows out a breath and his glower softens. "Eddie's my bestie." Confusion flicks over my face and he chuckles, "Eddie's what I call her, have since we were kids. Her name's Edith and she likes to be called Edie, so naturally I call her Eddie." He smirks at me and I nod my head in acknowledgement but stay silent, willing him to carry on.

"Lockheart was hitting on her. I know he was doing it to annoy me, but Eddie didn't. She blew up on me thinking I was being overprotective, but I'm really just looking out for her. She's too good and smart to be with some soccer player."

His eyes glaze over and a little smile forms on his face. This kid's in love with his best friend.

"Are all footballers off limits for her?" I ask, and have to hold my hands up in surrender at the dangerous look he throws my way. "Shit, that came out wrong. I meant you, Bro. Is she too good and smart for you?"

His face turns from angry to conflicted and he grabs the back of his neck. "Me and Eddie aren't like that. She looks at me like I'm family."

I nod my head at him, "I wouldn't be so sure. Think about it."

He rolls his eyes at me but I can see the intrigue in them. He likes her.

"Anyway, it's your turn, Marcello. Spill."

"Nothing as interesting as yours, I'm afraid. I'm trying to think of a theme for the fancy dress element of Charlie and Zoe's engagement party and I'm coming up with nothing that hasn't been done already."

I lean against the railings of the treadmill and fold my arms over my chest.

"You guys don't have proms over here do you?" He asks me, mirroring my stance.

I shake my head at him, "Not really. I think the schools do them now when you leave but not like you guys do."

"So what if you do a corny prom theme like under the sea or famous couples through the years. Me and my brothers went to those. I went stag to my prom. I couldn't take who I wanted to so I didn't take anyone."

A pang of sadness hits me for him. He's away from home and pining for the one person he thinks he can't have. Charlie and I need to look after him more. No wonder he's hitting the headlines for all the wrong reasons.

"Good job. You'll be at Charlie's party. You can come to this prom and dress like a famous couple because I fucking love that idea. And invite Edie as your plus one like you wanted to before." He starts to protest but gives up and just shakes his head at me. "And maybe leave the wannabe WAGs alone for a bit as well mate. They're not helping your cause with her."

He sighs at me, nodding his head, "Amen, Brother. No more headlines from me. The boss man already ripped me a new one. So did Eddie."

And with that he puts his earbuds back in and starts the treadmill up. I do the same thing. My mind's formulating the perfect plan to help me win Cleopatra's attention but I won't execute it until I've made her sweat for a little bit longer.

CHAPTER 12

Cleo

Well that was a week from hell. Helping to sort out your baby sister and best friend's relationship problems whilst knowing you've fucked up your friendship with your client/footballer/whatever else he should be labelled as, is a real mood killer. I've had to put a fake fucking smile on in front of my family all week, and to top it off, I haven't heard from Antony. I know I should've gone after him and apologised right away, but I couldn't let Juliet and Connor know I was worried about upsetting him. Especially not after she was using my feelings for him against me already. In front of them, he had to remain as Twatface, the annoying client and nothing else.

I need to figure out what this thing is with Antony before I throw my family into the mix. Once us Coopers bring someone into the fold it's near impossible to get rid of them. It's going to be hard enough to deal with losing him when he's had enough of me, let alone having six other people being broken-hearted as well. I wouldn't be able to deal with the embarrassment of it all in front of them.

I've just got home from a family dinner at Nell's where I volunteered to dress up as Wednesday Addams for Connor's

Halloween themed birthday celebrations in a few weeks. Juliet's with Connor, Emilia's with Marcus, Nell's with Will and I'm home alone. Again

Fucking Antony. Before he came along I wouldn't have minded being alone. I'd have enjoyed it. I would've cracked open a bottle of wine, dug out a Lucy Score or Annie Dyer book and savoured the peace. My guilty pleasure is reading romance stories with guaranteed happily ever afters. Will's the only one who knows about it though. To everyone else I only read thrillers. I can't have my Queen of Darkness reputation tarnished by public knowledge of my love of gushy love stories.

But now? I'm lonely. I want to be able to roll my eyes at some ridiculous thing Antony said. I want to be able to laugh at his oddness. I want him. I miss his incessant texts about nothing. I miss him asking me to meet him about 'work' related things. I miss him and I don't want to miss him.

Stomping over to the sofa, I flop down and turn the TV on. I need noise to drown out the silence in the room and the thundering thoughts in my head. After flicking through the guide three times and still not finding anything I want to watch, I switch it off again. Silence resumes around me. I grab my phone to see if any new messages have come through, but there's nothing.

I walk into my bedroom and grab the easel from under my bed. After placing my painting coveralls on, I set the canvas up with tubes of paint on the side and take a deep breath. Squirting some paint onto my palette, I dip the brush in it and just let go. I banish all thoughts from my mind and just let the paintbrush fly. Vibrant yellows and greens score the canvas.

After an hour of being immersed in my work, the ding of an incoming message distracts me. I take a deep breath, trying to slow down my rapidly beating heart. It's not him, Cleo. It's probably Marcus or Emilia trying to get you to go get drunk with them. With a disheartened sigh, I wipe my hands on my thighs so I can grab my phone. I look at the screen and see a message from Twatface and panic starts to swell in the pit of my stomach. Is he going to say he doesn't want to work with me anymore? That he doesn't want to see me again? I take a deep breath and open up the message.

Twatface: I know it's been a week since we've spoken but you can still bow down to me as I have the perfect theme for the party x

Cleopatra: I won't be bowing down to anyone, ever, thank you. Is it better than red hearts?

Twatface: Oh my little Sunflower, it's perfect. I've already spoken to Zoe and Charlie and they love it x

I've spent the last week feeling like absolute shit for upsetting him and he isn't even bothered about what happened? Well fuck you, Antony. Two can play at that game.

Cleopatra: Are you going to tell me so I can start to execute everything? The vendors are all waiting for my go ahead. Everything's been on pause for a week now...

Twatface: "Love Throughout The Ages"... everyone comes with a plus one and they dress up as a famous couple x

Twatface: You're welcome Sunflower (blowing kiss emoji) x

Cleopatra: I don't hate it. If Zoe's on board, I'll get started with everything.

Twatface: That's it? x

Cleopatra: That's it.

Twatface: Okay. I'm listening.

Twatface: Thank you, Cleo. Let me know if there's anything you need my assistance with regarding the party.

Shit. That wasn't what I wanted. He called me Cleo, not Cleopatra or Sunflower and there was no x at the end. He told me before that he's always listening, even when I'm silent. He's read between the lines and is being businesslike too. And I fucking hate it.

What's wrong with me?

I put the phone down and go back to my painting. I stretch my neck from one side to the other and fling my hands out to shake the tension loose from them. I pick up the brush and let my hands do what they need to. Gone are the yellows and green and in their place are browns and golds. I go with the flow and let my hands create whatever they want. It's been such a long time since I painted that I forgot what the feeling of being lost in the colours was like. This is what I needed. Not texts from my client.

After a long time, I place the brush to the side and zone in on my new creation. Eyes the colour of whiskey with gold flecks in them stare back at me, surrounded by sunflowers and red hearts. What the actual fuck? As I continue to scrutinise them, I scold myself for capturing Antony's bloody penetrating stare so well. How did I not know I was painting this? I grab the palette and brush and stomp into my bathroom to clean them up. I scrub at my hands, all the while cursing myself for being a twat over this whole thing.

I need help.

I need advice.

I need Emilia.

She's the one person I know that will give me honest advice. Plus she's the best secret keeper in the whole damn family. I stalk back into the bedroom, avoiding the fucking painting at all costs, take off the coveralls, and grab my phone. I bring Emilia's name up and hit call.

"Cleo? What's the matter?" She gets straight to the point and I love her for it.

"I need to talk to you, Em. On your own. I need it to stay between us. Please?"

I hate that my voice quivers slightly when I say please to her. Her sharp intake of breath tells me she heard it too.

"I'm on my way. Stick the kettle on. I'll be there in five minutes."

~

With a cup of tea in her hands I drag Emilia into my bedroom and show her the painting.

"What do you see, Emilia?" I ask her with my arms folded over my chest and a frown on my face.

She smiles at the painting and then quickly schools her face into its neutral state. "That you're painting again and you're better than I remembered."

I inhale through my nose, trying to calm myself down. "Not what I meant, Emilia, and you know that. Cut the shit please, Sis."

She chuckles and puts her hand up in surrender. "Okay. I see Antony's eyes surrounded by sunflowers and red hearts. You obviously see this too, so what's the real problem here and can we please leave your bedroom. After hearing the stories of your sexcapades, I feel unclean just being in here."

I laugh as we head back into the hall and then the living room. "They weren't that bad." I defend myself but she gives me a pointed look and I laugh again. "Okay, there were a couple that were on the raunchier side, but a lot of those were made up to gross you out."

Turning to face me before sipping her tea, she raises one sculpted brow at me. "You brat."

She elegantly sits down and deftly crosses her legs, one over the other, and places her tea on the coffee table. "What's the problem, Cleo?"

I huff out a breath and flop down next to her, as far from elegant as I can, making her roll her eyes at me. I may be in distress but it's still fun to mess with my older sister.

"I don't know what to do, Emilia. I like Antony, but I don't want to like Antony. He irritates the fuck out of me. But I like spending time with him. He makes me miss him and I hate him for that. He kissed me and it was the best damn kiss of my life. Why did it have to be so good? He is so bloody annoying. I want things with him that I've never wanted before, but I don't want to want them. Especially not with him, Em. Help me. Tell me some really bad things about him. Go."

I look at my sister, desperately willing her to come up with anything that will make the want and yearning in my heart go away.

"I don't think I can, Sis. I get the whole irritating thing. He is THE most annoying man on the planet. But he's also kind, considerate, and seems to genuinely care about you, Cleo. Why did you say 'especially not with him'?"

Emilia's gaze is unwavering, and normally I can withstand anyone's stare, but not hers and not now. I quietly tell her. "He's a footballer."

Panic rises up my throat and stops me from speaking. She reaches over to me and grabs my hand, squeezing it tightly. I swallow the lump of emotion down and finally spill my soul about Alex to someone in my family.

"In university I was dating a guy from the campus football team. He asked me out a lot and I said no a lot. I was friends with him and a few others on the team. I knew how they treated girls. I thought Alex genuinely liked me because he chased me so damn much. I eventually said yes to him and we dated for seven months. I thought we were okay together, nothing to write home about but he told me he loved me. He'd get me flowers and send me ridiculous teddy bears that had his voice recorded in them telling me he loved me. Everyone raved about how romantic he was, and instead of enjoying it, it irked me."

She chuckles and tells me, "Dad would be proud with 'irked.' Proceed."

I roll my eyes and carry on, still clasping her hand tightly. "He knew I loved sunflowers but he would only buy me roses because *he* thought they were more romantic. And it looked better, him carrying roses through campus. Then if I moaned about it, which I did because I'm me, I was ungrateful. In the end I shut up and started to believe him, stopped expressing my opinion because it was easier than arguing and hearing how unappreciative I was. I couldn't keep my snark in check for long though, and every now and then it would come out and he'd get upset and offended and I'd have to grovel and apologise. I was an idiot."

I shake my head at my stupidity. The humiliation at who I began to become back then reddens my cheeks. I want to curl up in my bed and forget about all of this, but I force myself to carry on, deliberately leaving out the part about not being built for relationships. I don't need Emilia to try to convince me differently.

"Anyway, I walked in on him fucking my flatmate. I was humiliated. Everyone on campus knew within days and I vowed I'd never go out with *anyone* again, definitely not a footballer. They're all the same. The Fucktwat's friend, Harry, was always fucking about with girls—at least he was honest about it though. And look at Antony's teammate Brady, he's in the headlines all the damn time.

"Antony can't be real. He's just enjoying the chase. If I gave in and we started a relationship together, eventually he'd get fed up with my snark and look elsewhere. It's what men do. I'd be left alone and humiliated on a much larger scale this time. I haven't stumbled upon the unicorn of the footballing world, Emilia. I'm not that special." A single tear slips down my cheek and I angrily scrub it away.

"Oh Cleopatra, I think you are and have, Babe. I'll come back to the wanker you just told me about in a second. But listen, I've been Antony's agent for years now. Do you want to know how many messes I've had to get him out of?"

I shake my head and she cackles back.

"None, Cleo. He hasn't been the serial womaniser, or cheating spouse, or the footballer who tries his luck with everyone. He's genuine. If anything, I've had to help him out for being too nice. He's the one people take advantage of, not the one that takes it. Listen to me, have I ever steered you wrong? Have I ever given you advice that wasn't good?"

I shake my head again and she rolls her eyes.

"Give him a chance and you'll see. Now this bellend you dated in university. Is this why you've held off on having a boyfriend? Why didn't you tell us when it happened?"

I lower my head and take my hand back from her. "I didn't want you guys to meet him because on some level I knew he wasn't right for me. After I dumped him, I didn't want you to know how stupid I'd been. I was so embarrassed. I did everything I swore I never would. I only started dating him because everyone was pairing off with people. Verity looked after me though. She found me ready to go off on the admin lady who wouldn't let me switch rooms and took me under her wing. She moved me into her place and about a week or two later Steve died and we were all so broken, I couldn't burden any of you with this crap…"

I shrug my shoulders and bite my lip to hold the emotions in place. I always get choked up when thinking of Nell's husband Steve, who was killed when Ben was only one.

Emilia grabs my hand back and rubs her thumb over the top of my hand. "I'm sorry we weren't there for you but I'm glad Verity was. Did you at least handle him in the correct Cooper way?"

I grin at her. "Oh, yeah. I told him just how shit he was in bed and then slept with a few of his teammates. I may have told them I'd never orgasmed with Alex and he may have been known as the guy that was a crap shag from then on. Lacy, my ex-flatmate, may have corroborated my story too. I guess she wasn't all bad."

She smirks at me. "Nice. So what did Antony do tonight?"

I frown as I pick my phone up and show her the texts. She smirks as she reads them and then settles back on the sofa and raises her eyebrow at me. "And?"

I blow out a breath and groan at her. "And, I don't like him being all businesslike with me. I don't like not liking that either, by the way."

She chuckles at me and sips more of her tea. "You know what you have to do, Cleo. You also know what you want. What's really stopping you?"

I look down at my lap as my hand comes up to twiddle with the sunflower charm on my necklace. It reminds me of the sunflower pin Antony wore on our 'work' date and sadness swims through me. "What if it doesn't work out? I'd have introduced him to everyone and then I'd have to deal with being sad and missing him and dealing with the family too."

Emilia sighs and tells me, "I know we do almost everything together, but you can have privacy from us too. Date him, stabilise your relationship and then introduce him to everyone. We're not going to judge you if it all falls apart, Cleo."

Reaching over, she places her hand on my knee and squeezes it.

"I have to text him back, don't I?"

I bring my head up and grimace at her smirking mouth and nodding head.

"Fine, but I'm not doing it with you here."

She laughs and gracefully uncurls her legs, standing regally. She's so bloody elegant. She reminds me of a ballerina, all prim and proper. She walks to the door and stops.

"What was that fucktwat's name from university again, Cleo?"

Caught off guard I answer her back.

"Alex Juliard." I pause as realisation sets in. "I didn't tell you that before, did I? Why do you want to know, Emilia?"

She smiles at me sweetly and tells me, "No reason, Sis. Goodnight."

Laughter peels out of me, not knowing exactly what she'll do but having a pretty good idea. I flop back onto the sofa cushions, grab my phone, and bite the bullet and text him, hoping he isn't as stubborn as me and won't hold a grudge.

Me: I'm sorry for calling you Twatface and for being rude. There, happy?

Twatface: Confused but not overly happy no, Cleo.

Me: I knew that wasn't going to be enough for you.

Twatface: Care to try again?

Me: Not really, no (swearing face emoji)

Twatface: Okay, Cleo.

Me: FINE!

Me: You're really annoying, do you know that?

Me: I'm sorry x

Me: I called you Twatface at first as I was keeping your identity secret because it's part of my job but also because I knew my family would freak out about who you were. Especially Connor and Will, they're big fans btw x

Me: I'm sorry I called you annoying just then as well, even though you really are x

Twatface:...

Me: (Eyeroll emoji) I'm sorry for not texting you after the incident at my office and apologising. I'm sorry for upsetting you, you didn't deserve it x

Twatface: Thank you, Cleopatra x

Me: We're okay? x

Twatface: Define okay? x

Me: Well you're calling me Cleopatra again and putting x's on the end of your texts. We're back to normal? x

Twatface: We're back to odd. I told you, I don't like normal, Sunflower x

I pause and look at my phone. A stupid smile slides over my face. I quickly scroll into contacts and change his name back to Antony. I roll my eyes at the feeling seeing his name on my phone evokes in me and scroll back to our messages.

Me: Do you want to meet for lunch tomorrow? To discuss work and everything? x

Antony: I know just the place. Shall I pick you up, Cleopatra? x

Me: Okay x

Me: It's annoying that I like seeing you using my full name so much. You're making me happy and irritated at the same time, is it any wonder I'm grouchy? x

Antony: (Laughing emoji) I wouldn't have you any other way, Sunflower. I'll see you tomorrow, Cleopatra x

Sweat is forming under my armpits and I'm thankful for the extra deodorant I put on as I nervously await Antony to pick me up. He's taking me to a restaurant he likes for lunch to discuss 'things'. I decided to wear a tight black pencil skirt

that hits just above the knee, a white shirt tucked in with a few buttons popped for a casual but smart look, and black converse. I didn't bring a coat with me because I'm an idiot and wanted to impress him. Cold and impatient, I hike my bag onto my shoulder and stop all movements when I spot his car.

Nerves flit through me, but so does happiness. I can't seem to get my feet to move, so Antony hops out of his car and opens the passenger side door, motioning with his hand for me to enter. Tears spring to my eyes and I bite my cheek to keep them at bay. I swallow the emotion that that one silly act of chivalry evoked and urge my feet to move.

When I reach him, he leans into me whilst gently taking hold of my elbow and kisses me on the cheek. The act is so sweet my breath catches in my throat. I step into the car and I'm thankful for the few seconds it takes for him to close the door and get back into the driver's seat next to me. Every-thing feels different with him today. More heightened. The air is crackling with electricity and I just hope it's the good kind.

As he puts his seatbelt on, I catch his gaze raking over my body and happiness spreads through me at the hitch in his breath when his eyes linger on my exposed cleavage. Ha, take that Antony, I cackle inside my own head. It's definitely the good kind of electricity. We drive in silence for a bit until I can't take it any more.

"So…"

Not the greatest start to a conversation, but at least I tried.

"So." He replies back with a smirk on his face.

"Why are you smirking?"

"I'm not." He replies, his smirk getting bigger until it turns into a full blown smile.

"You are, dipshit and now you're practically laughing. What's so funny, Antony?" I ask him as I cross my arms over my chest, making sure to lift my boobs up and squeeze them together even more. His gaze flits to me briefly and then back to the road, but not before the smile is wiped from his face and replaced by him biting on his bottom lip whilst frowning. And it's my turn to smirk.

"What did you ask, Cleopatra? Sorry. My mind went blank there."

Laughter bubbles out of my mouth and he turns his head slightly to me.

"What's so funny, Sunflower?"

I let the laughter subside before answering. "You are. You got distracted by my boobs. Admit it."

As we stop at a red light, he turns his head to face me and with twinkling eyes tells me, "They are very distracting, Sunflower. I want to do very naughty things with them and to them."

He stares into my eyes, then lets his gaze roam lower. Whilst he takes his fill of me, I squirm in my seat to try to stem my arousal. He notices and cocks an eyebrow at me as he brings his eyes back up to meet mine. This time, I'm the one biting their bottom lip as I look at him through my lashes. The air inside the car is filled with a voltage so high it could take out most of London. Our breathing intensifies. I lick my lips and love seeing his pupils dilate as he tracks the movement. He reaches over to touch my cheek and I'm lifting my hand to bring it to his face when a horn goes off behind us and brings us out of our lust addled fog.

"Shit! Cleopatra. You make me crazy."

"Right back at you, Twatface."

I grimace as I wait for his hurt puppy dog look but I'm pleasantly surprised when he starts to laugh instead. I shake my head and laugh with him. He reaches over and takes my hand and just like that, everything is back to odd with me and Twatface.

CHAPTER 13

Antony

Something's different about today. Cleopatra's different. It's like she's at peace with herself. And I'm not questioning it too much because I don't want to do anything to change it.

As we walk through the restaurant, hand in hand, I notice her occasionally looking up at me. She can't quite hide the little smiles she's trying so desperately to keep off her face. She's fucking adorable.

I'm a bit surprised when she suddenly drops my hand and takes a step away from me. When I bring my confused eyes up to see who or what's spooked her, I see Emilia standing with a man who's bouncing on his feet, a gleeful grin on his face.

"Fucking bollocks." Cleopatra bites out. I try to place my hand on her lower back to offer comfort, but she side steps me, anticipating my move. I force down the hurt and focus on the guy approaching us.

"Cleo, baby girl. Give Marcus some sugar."

Before jealousy rears its ugly head, realisation dawns on me as I hear his name. Marcus is Emilia's bestie and Nell's boyfriend's best friend. I hope I got that right. And if I recall, prefers Connor to any of the Cooper sisters.

"Hey Marcus. What are you guys doing here?" Cleopatra's voice sounds almost robotic. Like she's keeping her tone in check on purpose. Marcus lets go of her and turns his attention to me and I squirm under his perusal.

"Well aren't you a mighty fine specimen of a man. Please tell me you like peen?"

A bellow of a laugh erupts from my mouth as Cleopatra slaps her hand to her forehead and Emilia sidles up beside him.

"Boo, we've talked about this before," she scolds him and he pops his bottom lip out and pouts like a kid.

"But he's beautiful. He reminds me of Michele Morrone with a bit of Bucky thrown in for some added edge. Damn, Boy, you fine."

He links his arm with Emilia and I'm a bit taken aback at the warmth shining from her. She smiles lovingly at him and doesn't flinch away when he touches her. As I've only ever seen Shark at work, this is insightful for me.

"We're here to have a meeting, so if you'll excuse us." Cleopatra grabs my arm and tries to dodge around Marcus but he steps in front of her with a frown on his face.

"Erm, hell no. We can have lunch together. You can talk about work anytime. I want to get to know Twatface. This is Twatface, I take it?"

I nod and proudly tell him, "Yep, I'm Twatface. Nice to meet you. Cleopatra's told me a lot about you. Shark." I nod my head at Emilia who dips hers back to me. Marcus takes that as abject permission and turns on his heel to talk to the waiter about pushing two tables together.

Emilia steps closer to us and whispers, "I'm sorry, Cleo, he spotted you before I did. I haven't told him anything." She brings her eyes up and flits her focus between us and I'm not surprised at all when Cleopatra rolls her eyes at her.

"Just keep him in check, Em. I will throat punch him in

front of this entire restaurant if I have to," Cleopatra retorts. I chuckle but quickly stop as she narrows her eyes and bares her teeth at me.

Schooling her expression into one of complete control, she whisper-scolds, "You. Don't say a word about our kiss or about anything. Understand?" I grin and wink at her whilst nodding my head. She rolls her eyes again then turns away from me and stomps after Marcus.

I'm taking a second to watch her before following, when Emilia nudges me in the side. "Don't look at her like that or Marcus will know everything. And then so will everyone else."

"Is that a bad thing?" I ask, genuinely not caring if the whole world knows I want Cleopatra Cooper.

Emilia tilts her head to look at me. "Maybe not, Marcello. Maybe not."

"So how long have you two been together then? Miss Cleo is very tightlipped about the whole thing." Marcus bounces in his seat like an excited child and Cleopatra glares at him. Emilia smirks and I splutter into my drink.

I place the glass of water down and wipe my mouth on my napkin. "We aren't together. I'm just a client." Cleopatra shoots me a grateful look and then continues her glare at Marcus.

He grins at her and looks straight back at me. "But you are dating, aren't you?" His stare is relentless and I smirk because he's obviously spent a lot of time with Shark. But so have I.

I lean back in my chair and grin at him. "No, we aren't. In fact Cleopatra is quite adamant that she isn't now, nor would she ever want to date me, actually." I chuckle at her intake of breath and turn my head slightly to see her glare directed at me instead of Marcus now.

"But you want to though, right?" Marcus questions me.

I smile at him, "Abso-fucking-lutely."

I turn my gaze to Cleopatra and notice the pink hue spread across her cheeks. Immediately I feel bad for embarrassing her, but also happy that I'm pushing her out of her comfort zone a little.

"Cleo! What the duck is wrong with you? He's smart, good looking, and loaded. You, my girl, are a fool."

"Fuck off, Marcus. Like I'd take dating advice from you. One night stand advice? Most definitely. Dating, no way." Instead of looking hurt, Marcus grins mischievously at her and then holds his hand up for a high five. She slaps her palm to his and grins back.

"Seriously though, what's wrong with him? Does his peen curve? Because let me tell you girl, that can be an added bonus." He wiggles his eyebrows at me and I can feel my cheeks heat up. Cleopatra can't contain her laughter and spits the drink she's just sipped all over him. She cackles and splutters at the same time.

"Marcus, oh my fucking God. I love you, Dude. You made him blush. I owe you big time." I frown at her and then grin as Marcus mops the liquid off his face.

"Anything for the Coopers. My hot, growly Connor is included in that and we all know I'd do anything for Will too. Tony, you're included in that as well now. Welcome to the Cooper Clan. It's a high privilege, use it wisely."

Before I can respond, Cleopatra blows out a breath of air, stands up and heads toward the bathroom. Mumbling her excuses to us.

"Shit. Is she okay?"

Emilia nods her head at me. "She's fine. Just overwhelmed. I'd know if she was upset."

"So are either of you going to tell me the truth now? It's obvious you're dating or doing the horizontal tango together. Why doesn't Cleo want people to know? Is this because of whatever happened to her in Uni?" I stare at Emilia, not knowing what to say or do, and wait for her cue.

She takes a deep breath, places her palms on the table, and stands. "Well so much for that being a secret." She points at me. "You, fill Marcus in on what's happened between you and Cleo. He's loyal to a fault. He'll be able to help. And I think you're going to need all the help you can get with her." Then she points at Marcus. "And you, this is a secret still. She can't know about this. I'm invoking the Cooper circle of trust." She looks pointedly at both of us and then turns her gaze back to Marcus who holds his pinky finger out for her. I watch amazed as Shark, the cut throat boss, extends her pinky and wraps it around Marcus's. She offers me her other one and I'm frozen to my seat, unsure whether I should do this or not. But when she sighs loudly and raises a brow, I quickly offer my pinky too. Once we've forged our pinkie alliance, she stands straighter, smooths down her skirt and says, "Excuse me," and follows in the direction her sister went, leaving me at the table with a significantly more sombre Marcus.

"Do you really think she's okay?" I ask as I watch her head toward the bathrooms.

Marcus nods his head. "Yep. They have the Cooper Circle of Comfort. It's like a telepathy that tells them when a sister is in turmoil. Don't worry, she's fine. Now, spill the tea."

"Erm, what tea?" I ask, confused as anything right now.

He rolls his eyes, sighing loudly and dramatically. "The tea is... Never mind. Tell me what's going on."

"So..." I quickly fill Marcus in on where we are so far,

leaving out the information about Cleopatra's ex as that's not my story to share.

"Okay. We need the Cooper Clan Collective's help here. We've already helped Nell, Will, Connor, and Juliet, so now we need to help you two. Hmmmm." He frowns as he ponders on what he can do to help us and I fiddle with the napkin on my lap.

"That's cute." I look up ready to ask him what he's talking about, when I see him pointing to the sunflower pin I'm wearing.

I grin and tell him, "Oh this? I know Cleopatra likes them. Makes me feel like she's near even when she isn't." I smile shyly and he beams a wide smile back.

"What if you come to Not Hemsworths Halloween themed birthday party? That way you can meet everyone in a group social setting rather than as Cleopatra's boyfriend—it'll take the pressure off of her. Once she sees how much we all like you and that you slot into our little clique, she'll be less worried about dating you. I'll sort your costume out for you. How tall are you?"

He narrows his eyes and I smile nervously. "Six foot three. Who's Not Hemsworth and why is his birthday Halloween themed when it's March?"

"Perfect height for what I have in store. Standing next to Cleo's teeny self, you'll definitely look right." He grabs his phone and starts to type furiously on it and then places it down on the table and frowns as he tells me, "Because they wouldn't let me celebrate Halloween properly. We had to sort the gender reveal party instead so I got Halloween moved back a few months for Connor's birthday. It was an ordeal, but I managed it," Marcus tells me nonchalantly, and like he hasn't just implied that he is rather like a big kid. Before I can respond to anything he's just told me he carries on, "Don't worry, it'll all be fine. Give me your phone." Hesitantly, I slide my phone over to him and watch as he types his number in.

Suddenly a thought dawns on me. "You're the costume guy. The one who sorted everything for Ben's superhero birthday?"

He smiles widely and tells me, "That's me. Cleo's been talking about my mad skills, I see."

I frown at his use of 'mad skills' and he laughs loudly whilst handing me my phone back.

"Oh you'll fit in alright. Don't worry, I heard it and I won't use 'mad skills' again. For ducks sake."

I'm just about to ask him about the duck business when the ladies come back to the table. Emilia remains standing whilst Cleopatra sits next to me.

"Come on, Boo. I need to go. Let's leave them in peace." Marcus pouts a little but jumps up and winks at both of us. "Marcello, you're paying for our lunch," Shark calls out to me over her shoulder as they walk away and I chuckle at her boldness.

I look down at my phone and see Marcus has programmed his number in and sent himself a message from me—a gif of a dancing man in a unicorn onesie. I smirk.

"What's so funny?" Cleopatra asks me.

I smile and take her hand. "Nothing, Sunflower. I was thinking, we haven't decided on our costumes for the engagement party."

"I'm not dressing up. I'm there working, Antony." She tells me.

I mimic Marcus's pout. "But it's famous couples through history and everyone has to have a plus one. You're mine. We were going to go as The Antony and Cleopatra." I whine at her.

"Take Marcus, he'll dress up with you," she tells me with a grin on her face as I frown back.

"Listen, about Marcus, I'm sorry if I embarrassed you but I had to tell the truth. I do want to date you. More than anything."

She lowers her lashes and takes a deep breath.

"Me too. But I can't deal with all of that." She waves her hand in the direction her sister and Marcus just went. "Not yet. If they knew I was dating you, the questions, the teasing, it'd be never ending. I want to get to know *us* as a couple before I introduce you to *them* as my boyfriend. There's less pressure that way. Does that make sense?" she asks nervously and I squeeze her hand.

I know there's more to it. I know she's worried she isn't the right fit for me, that she can't give me the forever kind of love I crave, but it's my job to prove her wrong.

"Perfect sense. I can hear what you aren't saying, Cleopatra. Remember I'm always listening." She smiles at me so I lean over and place a kiss on her cheek.

If she needs time to get used to the idea of me being part of her life, that's fine, but I'll also show her just how well I can fit into her life whilst waiting. Hopefully with the help of all of those she holds dear, or the Cooper Clan Collective as Marcus called them.

CHAPTER 14
Cleo

I'm swamped with work. Juliet is swamped with work. And so is Connor. This should be a good thing, but it means I haven't had the chance to see Antony for a real date yet.

Or get to the bottom of Juliet's 'I'm fine' routine. The backward and forward dance between her wanting and not wanting Connor is driving me mad and I'm on my last nerve with her. I'm having to grit my teeth and bite my tongue to not erupt at her and her selfishness. The boy has told her, shown her how much he loves her, and yet she still doubts him. Connor deserves happiness more than anyone. So does Juliet. They deserve to be happy together.

Thoughts of their happiness bring my mind back to Antony. And our relationship. The man has made me happier than anyone I've ever met and that terrifies me. I've already become so dependent on him. I'm scared for when he isn't here anymore. I'm scared I'm going to be heartbroken. I'm scared of having to face my nearest and dearest and see the pity on their faces when he realises I'm not what he wants.

"Cleo?" Verity's voice screeches through my thoughts and I bring my gaze back to the computer where her face is staring at me, puzzled.

"Sorry. I zoned out. What did you ask?"

"I didn't ask anything. I just told you I sent over the modified to do list for the engagement party. What's going on with you?"

I blow out a breath as I admit, "I have a date tonight."

At least I'm rectifying one of my problems.

She screams like a banshee and I cover my ears, shushing her.

"I'm sorry, but you've never called your shenanigans a date before, which means this must be a real date. With who? What are you wearing? Where are you going?"

I roll my eyes at my friend's over-enthusiastic reaction and begrudgingly tell her, "With Antony. Don't moan at me, I know he's a client."

She grins. "If you told me you didn't find that man attractive and you weren't going to date him I would've been super ticked off at you. As it stands, I'm super happy instead."

I shake my head but grin too. "He's taking me out for a surprise but told me to wrap up warm, so I have no idea what to wear."

"Why do you seem so down in the dumps about a gorgeous, rich, super nice guy taking you out? Talk to me, Bestie."

I sigh and drop my head into my hands. I keep it there as I tell her, "I really like him, V. Like, really, really like him. What if it all goes tits up? What if it all ends badly? My family will fall in love with him immediately—they're meeting him in a few weeks' time at Connor's birthday— and then they'll be heartbroken when he leaves. And imagine the pity. If you think uni was bad, my family will be even worse. Nell will go into smother mode, it'll be awkward for Emilia having to work with him after she's threatened and possibly caused actual bodily harm to him, and Juliet will want to cry and cuddle me. By the way, they don't know we're dating, so don't tell anyone. It's all fucked up already."

Verity laughs softly and I bring my head up to watch her. I miss my friend more than anything, but I love seeing her so happy.

"IF anything bad happens, your family will get over it. Why are you so convinced it'll go wrong? Is this because that fucktwat at uni told you that you weren't built for relationships? If so, that's absurd. You've had a relationship with me for longer than I care to admit, and with Connor even longer than that, so stop being silly."

I bring my head up completely and give her a little smile. "That's a different kind of relationship and you know it."

She shakes her head at me. "No, it's not really. You love me, you put up with my bad habits, you tolerate my annoying traits, and you didn't murder me when we lived together and I messed everything up as I went. What was it you called me? The walking tornado?" She cackles and I laugh with her.

"That is true, but I did want to kill you a lot of the time. You're so damn messy."

"Ah, I know zis also." JP's voice filters through the screen and Verity frowns at him then smiles like all of her Christmases have come at once.

"I'm assuming he flashed you."

"Yes he did. He is so naughty." She giggles as a blush creeps over her freckled cheeks.

A smile spreads across my face at her happiness and a yearning creeps into my chest. I want that too.

"Anyway, my point was, you are so built for relationships, Cleo. You'd be the best girlfriend to the right person, and I think Antony might just be that person. So stop thinking about the negatives and start enjoying the positives. What will be, will be. Enjoy yourself." Her eyes flit to the side again and I smirk.

"Go play with JP. I'll keep you posted about the date and the party. Love you." I sign off before she can respond and find myself thinking about what she said.

Start enjoying the positives.

Fuck it, I'm going to do just that. Whatever happens between us is going to happen whether I like it or not. I don't seem to have any self control when it comes to Antony anyway, so it's time to start enjoying myself before it's too late.

CHAPTER 15

Cleo

I pull on my black leather-look trousers, red thigh-high boots, and black wrap-over top. Looking over my reflection in the mirror, I like what I see. The heel of the boots gives me a little extra height and my top is open enough to flash some cleavage. Perfect for what I have in mind.

I'm sticking to my guns of enjoying our time together, and I plan on driving him wild on this date. I want him to want me so much he stops being the gentleman he seems to be and starts acting like the beast I hope he is. God, I'm so turned on just thinking of him. I've basically exhausted my vibrators to images of us together, and although I come, it's never enough. Hopefully after tonight Antony and I will both be satisfied.

Nerves start to bubble in the pit of my stomach but I force them away. I have no time for nerves right now. I apply another coat of mascara and tousle my black hair that I've styled into waves for tonight. I'm getting ready in Emilia's apartment as Juliet is home and I don't want her to see me getting dolled up. She'll blab it to everyone. She's the worst liar ever and can't keep a secret if she tried. Emilia is out with

Marcus so I have the place to myself. She made me pinky promise I wouldn't have any kind of relations in here, and I won't. Pinky promises mean something to me.

The buzzer rings out in the empty apartment and causes me to jump. "Shit. Get yourself together, woman." I mutter as I walk to the intercom. "Hello?"

I sigh when I hear, "Sunflower" breathed back to me. He already knows this is Emilia's apartment from when he sent the hamper. He also knows I don't want Princess to see us together yet and that's why we're meeting here. I take some steadying breaths before he gets here and in no time at all there's a gentle knock on the door.

I open it and the breath catches in my throat. Dressed in tight black jeans and a mustard coloured jumper that's moulded to his perfect body, he looks damn good. I bite my lip and let my eyes roam over him, only stopping when I hear him groan.

"Damn, Sunflower, if you don't stop looking at me like that, we aren't going to make our date."

My gaze jumps to his. Flames of desire flicker in his eyes and I've never wanted to get burned so badly before. I lick my lips and smirk when his eyes follow the pink tip of my tongue as it caresses my bottom lip. I take a few steps closer to him, press my body up against his, and stand on my tiptoes so that my face is mere inches away from his.

"What would we be doing instead, Antony?"

I bite my bottom lip as he growls "*fuck it.*"

One of his hands is in my hair, the other wrapping around my waist. His lips are pressed against mine. I shiver when his tongue presses against the seam of my mouth, demanding entry, and when I moan he uses it to his advantage and caresses my tongue with his. My body is screaming for him. My head, my heart, my pussy, they're all calling for him. I can't think of anything but Antony. The way I want him, it's more than a physical thing. It's a need from deep within my soul crying out to his with the knowledge that we fit together, the missing pieces for each other's puzzles. The need for him to claim me as his. To make him mine. To know that I've made this man lose all sense of control. I need this more than I need air to breathe, more than I need sunflowers or snark. I need Antony Marcello more than I need to protect my heart.

That thought sobers me and brings me back to reality with a jolt. The nerves I banished earlier come to the forefront of my mind and I break away from his lips, pushing against his chest to get some distance between us.

He holds me tighter and bends his head so that he can look into my eyes. "What happened, Sunflower? Where did you go?" Concern is etched across his face and guilt threatens to swallow me whole.

"Nowhere. Things got a little hot and heavy there. That's all. I promised Em that we wouldn't do anything in her apartment." I smile at him, the fake smile I reserve for my annoying clients, and push against his chest again. "I need to fix my lipstick now, after you ruined it."

He grips me tighter, gazes into my eyes one last time, and then lets go of me. The sudden loss of his touch almost has me toppling off my heels, but thankfully I grab onto the kitchen counter and reach over to get my lipstick out of my bag.

I head into the bathroom to fix my lips and give myself a second or two. As I switch the light on and look at my reflection, I notice whiskey and gold flecks staring back at me.

"Antony, you're supposed to give a girl a minute to fix her makeup without you watching."

He smiles and steps closer to me. His front pressed against my back. His hands at his sides so his body is touching me but his hands aren't. He dips his head so that his chin rests on my shoulder and he watches me in the reflection of the mirror.

"I like watching you, Cleopatra. I like being near you. I like touching you and I definitely like kissing you. Can you feel how much I like kissing you?"

I gulp as his erection presses into me and nod my head, words are lost to me right now.

"Good. I like being the reason you need to take a minute. I like being the reason you're questioning everything in that head of yours. And I like seeing your lipstick smeared because of my kisses." He kisses me on the cheek, lingering to inhale my scent, and then turns and walks out of the bathroom.

That could possibly be the sexiest moment of my entire fucking life.

"I can't believe you brought me here, Antony." I snuggle into him, his arms wrapped around my shoulders.

He kisses the top of my head. "There was nowhere else I could bring you that was special enough."

I smile up at him, then raise my eyes further and look out to the stars through the open thatched roof of Shakespeare's theatre, The Globe. The round building that wraps around the stage is magnificent. Seats for the richer people and standing space for the poorer, well that's how it was back in the Elizabethan era. It's one of my favourite places in the world. My mum and dad would bring us here when we were little. We would wander around Southwark and then head over to catch a play. Always standing, as my mum said it enhanced the experience. How did he know?

A thought comes to me and I untangle myself from his arms. I stand in front of him with my hands on my hips.

"Antony, did Emilia tell you about this place? How we used to come here as kids with our parents? Did she tell you to bring me here? This isn't fair. You can't go behind my back and do things like this." I'm irrationally angry at him but I'm pulled back to reality when he frowns back at me and I think I actually hear him growl.

"No, I didn't talk to her. I saw the way you were captivated by Antony and Cleopatra. I watched your eyes dance with happiness at the words that I couldn't understand. Saw the way you slid closer to the edge of your seat the further the play went on. I thought what better place to take you than the actual theatre that Shakespeare had his plays performed in. You told me not to tell Emilia anything. And I haven't. When are you going to understand that I'm listening to you?"

He drags his hand through his hair and blows out a breath. I tentatively reach out to him and he reluctantly lets me take his hand.

"I'm sorry, Antony. I guess I'm just waiting for the bubble to burst with you." I admit shyly lowering my gaze.

He lifts his hand to my chin and raises my head so I'm back to looking up at him. "Never lower your head to me. You're my Queen, Cleopatra. If you lower your head, your crown slips and we can't have that."

He traces my mouth with his thumb and my core clenches in need for him. I let my tongue peek out through my lips and softly touch the tip of his thumb. He groans, letting his hand slide to the base of my neck where he wraps his fingers around the back of it. He pulls me closer, brushing his lips over mine. He kisses me under the stars, in the middle of The Globe, with people surrounding us, and I don't want him to ever stop. I want him. Not for tonight. Not for a little while. But forever.

I bring myself closer to him, needing to feel him against all of me. I try to take the kiss deeper but he breaks away.

"Cleopatra, that's not happening on our first real date."

"Who says?" I ask boldly.

He grins at me and raises an eyebrow. "I do."

When the trumpet fanfare rings out to signify the play is starting, I spin away from him and grab his hand. "We'll see Twatface, we will see."

CHAPTER 16

Down and dirty – Texts

Cleo: I can't believe you said no to getting down and dirty with me. Are you sure you don't like peen? x

Antony: Quite sure, Sunflower. I think you felt how sure in Emilia's bathroom earlier on x

Cleo: I did (Purple devil emoji) x

Cleo: Why did you say no, then? I was a sure thing Antony (winking emoji) x

Antony: LOL

Antony: Do you say that to all the boys, Sunflower? x

Cleo: Only the ones I like (winking emoji) Never been turned down before though x

Antony: From now on you only say it to one person, Cleopatra. No one else x

Cleo: Ooh I like this side of you. Are you jealous? x

Antony: Jealous of anyone that's touched you? That's had your lips pressed against theirs? That knows what you look like naked? Knows what you look like when you come? Knows how good your pussy feels wrapped around their dick? Yeah, Sunflower. I'm fucking jealous. So jealous it drives me crazy x

Cleo: Shit, Antony. Now I'm hornier than ever and alone. Thanks for that Twatface x

Antony: My pleasure. Think of me (Purple devil emoji) x

Antony: I had the best time tonight. Date number four was a success, no? x

Cleopatra: Erm well let's see shall we? x

Cleopatra: You took me to mini golf which was fun. But not what I had in mind x

Cleopatra: You see, Antony, I wore some very sexy lingerie under my outfit x

Cleopatra: I thought you'd enjoy unwrapping me…

Antony: I. DID. NOT. KNOW. THAT…

Cleopatra: There were clasps…

Cleopatra: Garters…

Cleopatra: Bows…

Cleopatra: Laces… all waiting for your fingers to undo them x

Antony:…

Cleopatra: *Whispers* There were stockings attached to my garter x

Antony: It's not too late… x

Cleopatra: Goodnight, Antony x

Cleo: I'm so sorry I couldn't meet you tonight. Shit hit the fan with my stupid sister and Connor needed me x

Antony: It's okay, Sunflower. Zoe told me what happened over dinner between Juliet and Connor. Are you alright? x

Cleo: I will be once I kick Juliet's arse. She was so horrible to him, Antony. He didn't deserve the words she said to him x

Antony: I know. Hopefully this is just a bump in the road for them both. Do me a favour though? x

Cleo: What? x

Antony: Don't beat her up. She's your sister and you love her. Let her know you're hurt by her actions and make her see sense about Connor. Be the sister you've always been to her. She's hurting too, even if it is by her own doing x

Cleo: You always know exactly what to say to make things better. That would've gotten you a blow job tonight had you not imposed a 'no sex' policy with us x

Antony: Blow jobs aren't a part of sex. You can swing by my house on your way to Juliets. I'm good like that (winking face emoji)

Cleo: I'm sorry, it's called oral sex for a reason and that would be against the rules. Night, Antony x

Antony: (Eyeroll emoji, blowing kiss emoji) x

CHAPTER 17

Antony

"Can you control the sweating please? You're ruining my makeup!" Marcus huffs, but I just grin at him.

"Sorry. I'm nervous. This is a big deal for me. It's the first time I get to meet everyone."

He rolls his eyes and grabs a mini fan off the side of his 'makeup trolley.' He switches it on for me and thrusts it toward my face. "Cool yourself down. I will not have your overactive thermoregulation system ruining my reputation as *THE* costume guy, Mr. Marcello."

A grin overtakes my face because he's deadly serious and is shooting daggers at me. But as he's wearing a bald cap, has no nose, and long bony fingers with sharp as fuck nails attached, so I can't help but smirk. I blow the cold air onto my face and take some deep breaths to try to stem the nerves that are bubbling inside of me. These are worse than any nerves I've felt before a match, even worse than the ones I had before I had to take a penalty for England in the European qualifiers last year, and I was terrified then. I felt the weight of a nation on my shoulders. Thankfully I smashed it into the back of the net and I'm hoping I'll do the same with meeting the family too.

I haven't seen Cleopatra for over a week. She's been swamped with work and family stuff, but we've spoken on the phone and through texts everyday. If I'd known on our last date that she was dressed up in sexy lingerie for me, I would've forgotten about the mini golf and the need to get to know her more before I made love to her. As it stands, my balls are still blue and my dick aches for her. The thought of her wearing garters and stockings for me sends a jolt of electricity to my dick, causing me to shift on the chair in order to relieve the ache in my balls.

I can't wait to see her. She's already sent me strict instructions about what I can and can't tell her family about us. She isn't comfortable with them knowing we're dating, and whilst that irritates the life out of me, I'll respect her wishes. For now. After tonight though, if all goes well, I'll be asking her to reconsider her stance on us. I don't want what we have to be a dirty secret. We've been dating for four weeks now. And have known each other for months. That's long enough for her to know I mean what I say. I haven't once let her down or gone back on my word so she needs to stop comparing me to that dickweed from uni. I'm building our relationship and trying to do what my papa told me to do. I'm letting her come to the realisation that we are meant to be together on her own.

"As much as I love that brooding, tortured look on that gorgeous face of yours, I also know it's not how you usually look, so spill, Marcello." Marcus interrupts my thoughts and I bring my gaze to him. "Don't try it. I've been around enough men that are hooked on Cooper women to know what that look means. What's going on?" He softens his tone and approaches me with his makeup in hand. "Close your eyes so I can do this but talk until I tell you not to."

"Are you not taking the fingers off and those nails? I don't want to have to go to the hospital because you've poked my eye out."

He sighs loudly, "I am an expert. Now close your bloody eyes and answer my ducking question."

I take a deep breath doing as I'm told. "I love her but I think it's too soon to tell her. I don't want to spook her."

The brush tickles over my face and I have to bite my cheek to stop my nose from twitching.

"I'm confused. The last time I saw you, you guys weren't dating. Has something changed? Has our little Cleopatra been holding out on us?"

I open my eyes quickly and almost get poked in the eye by some sort of brush.

"That's why I said close your bloody eyes. It won't be my nails causing you damage, it'll be your lack of listening skills. Jeez." Marcus scolds.

"Sorry. They're closed again. Marcus, I wasn't meant to say anything. She isn't ready for everyone to know. Please don't tell them. I don't want to ruin everything before I get the chance to tell her how I feel."

I hear him sigh then chuckle next to me. "Don't worry, my hot little Michele-Sebastian hybrid. I won't say anything. I will tell you that Emilia and I have been discussing this at great length and have already discussed the possibility of a little cloak and dagger dating going on. What's holding her back?"

It's my turn to sigh. I know she hasn't told everyone about Dickweed. I know she would hate me if I told them. I can't break her confidence anymore than I have.

"I think she's worried about what will happen if we don't work out. Introducing me as a friend is easier than a boyfriend. I'm hoping once she sees how I fit in tonight she'll relent and let me in a bit more."

I'm hit with silence and no movement but flinch as Marcus slaps my thigh and then grabs it and squeezes it repeatedly. "Wow, that's really hard. It's all muscle. Jeez,

Cleo's a lucky lady. You can open your eyes now." I do as I'm told and find Marcus tapping a long bony finger against his chin. "So we need to make sure you really fit in without telling everyone that you're dating. Shit, I'm going to help you and give you a crash course in all things Cooper. Buckle up, this is going to be fast. That sentence normally ends with 'and hard' but you don't like peen, so your loss."

As laughter bellows out of me, Marcus grins and begins to tell me all about the Cooper Clan.

Poised with all the Cooper knowledge that Marcus could squeeze in, I walk into Nell's house behind him and take a few calming breaths as we head into the kitchen. The chatter and laughter stops and I don't know if it's because of our costumes or because the infamous Twatface is here. After a few awkward seconds, a little kid in a black and white striped top with a white painted face and dark circles around his eyes comes bundling into Marcus's arms.

"You look awesome. I was a bit scared by you two." He beams at me. "I'm Ben, or Pugsley, but you already know dat cause you're my butler."

I grin at him as a woman dressed in a tight black dress turns around to face us, showcasing her bump as the fabric stretches across it. From behind you couldn't tell she was pregnant, but as she walks toward us, she's radiant. "Because, Ben. The word is because. Not cause." She grins at him and ruffles his hair. She turns her gaze to me and smiles. "Hi, I'm Nell, you must be Antony. It's lovely to finally meet you."

I reach out to shake her hand and frown at her. "This is so weird. You look a lot like Cleopatra, but with green eyes." I chuckle nervously. This is such a pathetic first impression with her oldest sister.

She giggles at me, "It is weird how much we look alike with this black wig on. Let me introduce you to Will, who is a huge fan by the way."

"My lady…" I hear a man groan out behind her and Marcus chuckles next to me.

"She totally blew your '*I'm not fussed by the hot, famous footballer in my kitchen routine*'."

"Shut up, Marcus," he snaps back.

Ben shrieks, "Oh no, Daddy said rude words."

My gaze flicks over to Will who grimaces as Nell tells Ben, "Don't worry, I'll make sure he puts money in the jar." She shoots daggers at him as he walks over to her and wraps his arms around her from behind.

"Cara Mia…" He kisses her neck as she giggles, slapping his hands that are resting on her huge baby bump. Their affection makes me smile. I crave that closeness they have with each other. Will Cleopatra and I ever get to that point?

"Nice to meet you, man. I am a huge fan. I'm Will." He holds his hand out for me to shake and I smile back at him.

"Nice to meet you, too. Congratulations to you both, by the way." I motion with my head to Nell's bump and they both beam back at me.

"Thank you. By the way this little lady is moving about it could be anytime." Nell's eyes are filled with love and happiness. I want to see that reflected back to me in Cleopatra's eyes. I want to be the one to make her eyes twinkle with love.

"A-hem. Sorry to break up this lovefest, but we need to go if we want to meet Connor and stop him from coming here before he's supposed to. Juliet's all set, we've left her in the bedroom." Cleopatra enters the kitchen and I spin on my heels. Her eyes meet mine and I don't miss the happiness and apprehension flash through them when she sees me.

"Hey, Cleopatra. Shark." I dip my head to Emilia and fight every urge I have to go over and kiss my Sunflower senseless. She looks gorgeous with her braided pigtails and black dress on.

"Shark? What's that about?" Nell asks as she grabs a bag.

"Don't ask, Nell. I wouldn't want to have to curse you. You are my sister after all." Emilia brings her wand up and points it in Nell's face. Clearly, she takes dressing up as seriously as Marcus, and dressed as his devoted Bellatrix, she's even fiercer than normal. Her wild black curly hair looks out of place with her complexion, but she fits the role she's playing perfectly. I can't wait to tell Charlie all about this, he will never believe this side of Shark exists. Who would've thought Shark would be a Harry Potter fan?

Everyone files out of the kitchen, but Cleopatra hangs back. She looks around to make sure we're alone and stands on her tiptoes to press her lips against mine. Instantly, my dick hardens in my pants and a growl rips from my throat as I wrap my hands around her waist, pulling her closer to me so our bodies are pressed together. Too quickly she pulls her lips away from mine. I hold her tighter in my arms and press my forehead to hers. "Sunflower, I need you. I missed you."

She tenses and then momentarily relaxes in my arms. "Come on. They'll be wondering where we are."

I let her go reluctantly but try to take hold of her hand. She moves away quickly and looks at me as we fall in step, side by side. "I'm sorry, if they see us…"

"So what if they do, Cleopatra?"

She shakes her head at me and mouths "not yet" as we walk outside and catch up with the rest of her family.

CHAPTER 18

Cleo

I know he's getting annoyed. I know he wants more from me. I know he wants me to tell everyone that we're together. But I'm fucking scared.

If I tell them, it makes what we have and what we're doing real. We become an actual couple. And with that comes the risk. The risk of everything crumbling around me and having to deal with the fallout when it does.

"I really like him, Cleo. Why aren't you dating him? He obviously likes you." Nell is cradling her bump as we sit on the bench opposite from where Ben is dragging Antony and Connor by the hands to the next house to 'trick-or-treat.' Nell has the best neighbours for going along with this in March. Marcus and Emilia stayed at the house to help Juliet set up for her grand gesture to get Connor back—because of course she fucked that all to hell again. I don't think she'll go through with Marcus's idiotic idea, but hopefully she'll put enough effort in that Connor will see she's serious about them being together.

"He's a client, Nell. He only came today because Marcus railroaded him into it and he's too much of a nice guy to say no." My tone of voice is flat. I'm deliberately hiding any emotion from it.

"Bullshit, Cleo. He's spent the entire evening with your family whilst shooting you pining, lovesick looks. Looks which you have been shooting back. Somethings going on with you two, now spill."

Emotion clogs my throat and I shake my head to clear it. "There's nothing going on. He's just my client." I watch as he picks Ben up and flings him over his shoulder. My nephew shrieks in happiness and a tear trickles down my cheek. Nell grabs my hand and squeezes it tightly.

"Listen, I don't know what's going on but I'm getting pretty annoyed at you girls hiding things from me. First Juliet, now you. I won't push you tonight, Cleo, but you need to remember us Cooper sisters work better together. When we try to do things on our own we fuck up. Just look at me and Juliet if you want proof." I lower my head to shield my eyes, hiding the pain and fear I know she'll easily read in them.

"Relationships. Love. They're worth taking the risk for, Cleo. I wouldn't be sitting here as big as a house if I hadn't taken the risk. You and Juliet forced me into it, remember?" I nod my head. We did force her into a confrontation with Will by setting them up on a date without them knowing. "And Juliet wouldn't be ready to bare her soul to Connor if you hadn't helped him fake date her to prove they should be together. You need to open up that heart of yours. I know you're the self professed Queen of Darkness, but let in some sunshine. Antony is your sunshine. The man's dressed up as a giant butler to fit in with our family themed costumes and is wearing a bloody sunflower pin for God's sake."

I laugh and cough at the same time and end up shooting spit out of my mouth onto Nell's knee. She looks down and giggles as I choke on my laughter even more. "Not the kind of bodily fluids I expected on my black dress tonight but anywho…"

With eyes as wide as saucers I shriek, "NELL! I did not expect that from you. Shit, Sis." I laugh at the red blush that creeps over her cheeks.

She blows out a breath.. "Well, sperm helps induce labour. And I really want her to be here now."

I smile at my sister, reaching over to rub her belly. "Not long now, Sis." I let my gaze sweep over to the boys and catch Antony's eye. He beams at me and winks and I smile back at him.

"Just a client, my arse." I hear Nell muttering next to me.

"I think this is a family thing guys, maybe I should go," Antony says as we pile into the waiting room of the hospital, desperate to see our new niece. As soon as Juliet had finished telling Connor what a twat she'd been—stamping her foot in true Princess style to make sure everyone got her point—our little niece decided she wanted in on the fun. Still in full costume, we all made our way to the hospital and are now eagerly awaiting newborn baby cuddles.

I roll my eyes at Antony and grab his hand. "You've been with us all night. Witnessed Princess's famous foot stamp and Marcus's pout on numerous occasions, you deserve to meet the newest member of this crazy family." He smiles down at me and I want nothing more than to snuggle into his side. Instead, I quickly drop his hand and adjust my braided pigtails. I don't miss the hurt that crosses his face and the smile he plasters on to cover it. I'm such a bitch. But I just can't take that leap yet.

We file down the hall in twos and I walk silently next to Antony. He has his hands firmly in his pockets, eyes looking straight ahead and I have a sinking feeling eating away at me. I know I'm pushing him away but I don't know how to stop.

We walk into the room and all thoughts of Antony are swept aside as I see my beautiful niece for the first time. Emotion wells inside of me as they tell us her name, Beatrice Connie Blake. A nod to my best friend and brother-from-another-mother. As everyone takes turns holding her, I wander over to Connor and perch on the arm of his chair.

"He's a good guy, Cleo. What's holding you back?"

I sigh as I turn to look at him. "I know. And I like him, Connor. I'm just scared it's not enough to just like someone. You have to trust them, to know how to work through the bad times together, and I don't think I can. Please don't ask me why." He looks at me, worry filling his eyes as I lower my gaze from his, afraid that if I look at him any more I won't be able to contain my emotions.

"You can learn how to do all of that, Cleo. Happiness is worth taking that risk. Believe me. You're one of the best people I know, you deserve to be happy, to be with someone who adores you. Don't give up on love because you're scared." He gets up and walks away before I can argue with him.

I am scared. Fucking terrified. Of Antony, of us, and how I'll be when it inevitably ends.

With goodbyes said we walk outside. Antony and I head to his car whilst Marcus, Emilia, Connor, and Juliet head to theirs.

I reach out to take Antony's hand once we're out of sight from them but he shifts away and runs his hand through his hair instead. "I can't keep doing this, Cleopatra. This hot and cold act, it's too much."

I look down, guilt consuming me.

"I want to tell them we're together. I want to shout from the rooftops that you're my girlfriend. We've been dating for four weeks and talking for a lot longer. Please, Sunflower. I'm begging you here. Let me in."

The desperation is etched in his voice, and I want to give in and tell him that we can tell everyone, but instead I choke out, "Not yet. I'm not ready…"

He blows out a breath, frustration dripping with his words as he says, "You won't ever be ready, Cleopatra. And I can't do this anymore." He walks around to the driver's side of the car and gets in. He lowers his head and rests it on the steering wheel. My heart is racing, I don't want him to leave but I can't give him what he wants. It's too much. But I want him. I'm about to dive into the car to be with him when a horn blares from behind me. I turn around and see my family in the other car and I look at Antony again. He lowers the passenger side window, "Go."

With that one word, I turn on my heel, striding toward my family and away from Antony. My heart is heavy but I was right at the beginning, I can't give him what he wants. He deserves the forever kind of love. I can't be the one to give it to him though.

CHAPTER 19
Antony

As I pull up to Charlie and Zoe's driveway, I spot my best friend waiting for me on his doorstep. I jump out of the car and fumble my steps when he jumps back and shouts, "What the fuck, Dude?"

It takes me a few seconds to realise I'm still dressed like a zombie/frankenstein butler and start chuckling at him. "Sorry, I forgot I was dressed like this. I look good though, right?"

"Too fucking good. Scared the shit out of me, man."

"Why are you out here...FUCK!" Zoe walks out and takes one look at me and screeches.

I laugh hard as Charlie wraps an arm around her shoulder. "It's just Antony, Baby."

She giggles as she brings her hand to her chest. "You scared the fuck out of me, Ant." This is why I love Zoe. She looks all prim and proper, but swears and burps with us like she's one of the lads. She's fucking perfect for Charlie.

"Sorry, Zo. I forgot I had this still on and then realised when I was halfway home I have no idea how to get this shit off."

She laughs and holds out her hand for me. "Come on. I have some good make-up remover that will have you back to your handsome self in no time. Charlie can grab you some clothes too."

"But he never gives me my clothes back, Babe." he whines as we all head into their house and I already feel my spirits lifting. This is what I needed. Time spent with my nearest and dearest while I try to figure out what the hell to do about the mess I made with Cleopatra.

"And I told her she'd never be ready and that I can't do this anymore. She went home with her family. I'm not expecting her to contact me, though. I should never have listened to Papa. I'm not built for these emotional games. I can't do sneaking around and hiding how I feel. I was surrounded by her family, two of her sisters in love and happy, and I just wanted to feel the same. I wanted to hold her hand and kiss her head and bring my arms around her. Fuck, I should've listened to you, Charlie." I drop my head onto his shoulder and sigh loudly. Zoe grabs my hand and holds it tightly.

"She seemed really sweet and lovely when we met the other day, but when her family showed up it was a massive shitshow, Ant. Maybe she just needs a bit of time."

"Nope. I disagree. If she's as close to her family as you say she is, she should want to tell them. You did the right thing. You don't deserve to be someone's secret. Maybe she's playing a game. Take advantage of the naive footballer. I don't know. But I won't stand back and see you get hurt on purpose." Charlie brings his arm up and places it around my shoulders. I want to argue with him, to protect Cleopatra's reputation, but an overwhelming happiness that I have him in my corner overtakes me. I grab him in a bear hug.

"You're the best brother an only child could ever have wished for."

He chuckles and Zoe giggles as well. "What will you do now?"

I shrug my shoulders, "I don't know. I love her, but I want more. I want what you guys have, what her sisters have, apart from Shark. Did I tell you she was dressed up tonight?" I turn my head to Charlie.

His eyebrows shoot up so they're almost touching his hairline, "As who?"

Zoe shakes her head then rolls her eyes and I'm reminded of Cleopatra again and the ache in my chest thuds harder.

I pull up my phone and show him a picture of Emilia and Marcus in full costume.

"Holy shit, Shark's smiling. Not her 'I'm circling my prey and ready to feast on them smile' but an actual full on smile." Charlie grabs the phone and examines the picture. A frown mars his face and I look over at the screen to see what he's looking at. A picture of 'The Cooper family' is staring back. Emilia took it before Nell went into labour and sent it to me. Everyone is looking at the camera except Cleopatra. She's staring at me. I can see the apprehension in her eyes but I can also see the love written on her face. Charlie can see it as well. His face softens and his tone of voice does too. "Let's just focus on the game tomorrow night. Training, first thing in the morning, will sort your head out. Let her stew for a bit and then decide what to do afterwards. She looks confused. I don't think she's doing this on purpose. Not anymore." He squeezes my shoulder as I nod.

Focus on the game, deal with Cleopatra after. I can do that. It gives me two days to let her figure her shit out. Hopefully it's long enough.

CHAPTER 20

Coopers Care - group texts

Connor: Fuck, that was a dirty tackle. Let us know you're okay, Marcello.

Will: Should've been a straight red. The ref's a wanker. Marcello, if you need anything, let us know.

Marcus: I was only watching for the thighs but damn even I know that was dirty.

Nell: Cleo, is he okay?

Nell: Is Cleo with him?

Connor: I think Princess said she was out. And was out last night too.

Nell: Are you with Juliet?

Connor: No, I'm not.

Nell: Well, where are you?

Marcus: With me, ogling footballers' thighs.

Connor: No, I'm not. I am with Marcus but I'm not ogling their thighs.

Marcus: Will says the same thing when we ogle men together. Always denying the truth (Eyeroll emoji)

Will: Shut up, Marcus.

Marcus: I'm showing Benvolio. You'll have to put more money in the jar.

Emilia: Great. When Antony does get to his phone, he will be inundated with messages from the less intelligent side of the Cooper family. Nell excluded.

Nell: You're lucky you put that. I may be in a 'lack of sleep, caused by your niece' induced fog right now but I'm still intelligent.

Will: I resent that, Emilia. Marcus drags my IQ down. You should know that.

Connor: Did you just imply Emilia is stupid because she's besties with Marcus? Oh you're in so much trouble, Will.

Will: Shut up, Connor. I didn't mean that, Emilia.

Marcus: Get him, Boo.

Will: Fuck off, Marcus. Emilia, you know I didn't mean that…

Will: Emilia?

Will: Shit, she's going to kill me isn't she?

Will: Fuck!

∼

The next morning

Connor: Em, you heard from our boy yet? It's been a while now.

Marcus: Antony, there is only room for one drama king in this group and I've called dibs on it. Contact us.

Will: Let us know if he's okay, oh great, wise, Emilia who has superior knowledge than I.

Connor: (Laughing emoji) Did she make you say that?

Marcus: She didn't, I did…

Will: WHAT? You told me she said I had to say it or she was going to hurt me. You said she was pissed…

Marcus: (Laughing hysterically emoji)

Connor: (Laughing hysterically emoji)

134

Emilia: I'm not complaining about the name change, Will.

Will: To Marcus (Middle finger emoji) Any news from him, Em?

Emilia: Nothing yet.

Juliet: @Cleo, have you heard from him?

Cleo: Heard from who? What's going on?

Marcus: Did you not see our texts last night?

Cleo: Nope. I muted you fuckers. I was out.

Juliet: Were you wearing your red boots?

Cleo: Yep.

Nell: I'm so disappointed, Cleo.

Juliet: Oh, Cleo.

Connor: Cooper…

Emilia: Cleo, can you make your way over to my office please. We need to talk.

Cleo: About what?

Cleo: Why are you disappointed?

Cleo: Emilia?

Cleo: Guys?

CHAPTER 21

Cleo

My stomach is rolling with nerves as I walk to Emilia's office. I've tried calling Juliet, Connor, Nell, and Marcus but they're all ignoring me. I know they're pissed off because they think I was out the last two nights. But I wasn't.

I lied to them. All of them.

I needed to be alone. I needed time to deal with my emotions before I answered their questions. I had to let the tears flow, let my heart break. I did exactly what I knew I would. I pushed Antony away.

I muted their bloody texts as soon as I saw his name mentioned. I didn't want him to know I was wallowing in self pity, alone, in my office. I didn't read those messages, swiped left and deleted the whole group chat. But I couldn't ignore Juliet outright asking me if I'd heard from him this morning. It would've made them all panic, especially as I ignored them last night.

I didn't want to deal with the Spanish inquisition from Juliet about what happened between me and Antony after we left the hospital. Juliet may be in a love bubble with Connor, but as soon as Marcus started questioning me about Antony, her interest was piqued. I managed to shut them down and told them he had to see his friend and that was why I was riding home with them. It was a lame excuse, but the only one I could come up with without showing them just how sad I was.

I knew Juliet wasn't fooled. She knew there was more to us, but she didn't push me in the car. She would wait until we were alone. So I went home and changed into my 'getting lucky' red boots then went right back out again.

These damn boots used to make me feel good about myself. But as I sat alone in my office, they just reminded me of all the times I wore them before. The insignificant hook-ups. Images of men dancing with me would flit through my head and I felt sick. I don't want that anymore.

A memory of Antony popped into my mind. Our first date, when he pressed up against me in Emilia's bathroom to show me just how excited he was. I was wearing them then too. The difference was I wanted his body against mine. I loved feeling how hard he was for me. With him, I felt beautiful and desired for more than my looks. I didn't need the damn boots to make me feel good about myself because Antony did that with a look or a smile. He made me feel like a Queen, and not of darkness. Just a Queen. His Queen.

I can't even pretend anymore, can't keep lying to myself. I want Antony. But I walked away from him.

I knock on the door of Emilia's office and she calls out for me to enter. Blowing out a breath, I put my sassy pants on as I stride inside.

"Did you miss me so much you had to summon me here, Sis?" I grin at her and she glares back at me. She raises an eyebrow and folds her arms over her chest, taking in the outfit from my previous night 'out.'

"Cleopatra, I'd like you to meet Charlie Bennett. He's a client of mine and yours. And Antony's best friend. Charlie, my sister and your party planner, Cleopatra. You'll be dealing with Charlie for the foreseeable future." Charlie stands up and reaches his hand out. I shake it tentatively, a frown marring my face.

"Where's Antony? Why am I working with Charlie now? Did he tell you he doesn't want to work with me? Is this a joke?" My confusion is turning to rage and even though I'm standing in front of a client, I can't contain it.

"No, he didn't. Cleo, listen to me. Antony was hurt last night."

Emilia's serious tone filters through my rage and it takes all of my strength to remain standing after hearing her words. He's hurt. Fuck. How bad is it? Is he going to die? Images of Steve flash in my head. Of the pain Nell went through at losing him. I can't lose Antony. Not now. My hand reaches out and grips the side of Emilia's desk. I stumble forward a few steps and plonk into the chair next to where Charlie is standing.

"I-i-is he dead?" I whisper. Tears are falling freely, cascading down my cheeks. Emilia rushes to my side and grabs hold of my hand. The need to touch me is too strong for her to ignore.

Her voice takes on a softer tone as she tells me, "He's okay, Cleo. He isn't dead. He got injured during his match."

I should feel relieved. It's just a football injury. But the dam breaks and the emotions I've been holding back for so long hit me all at once. I sag against her and sob. I cry for what happened to me in uni. I cry for Steve because I was never able to before. And I cry for Antony. For pushing him away. For denying what we had. For refusing to acknowledge my feelings for him. Once the tears subside, I take a deep breath and punch Emilia on the arm.

"Ow, you little brat. That fucking hurt."

"Good. You deliberately made me think he was hurt worse than what he was. You made me fucking cry over him. In front of his best friend." I glance at Charlie, who's grinning from ear to ear, narrowing my eyes. Instantly his grin disappears, he stands straighter and takes a step away from us.

"I had to. *He* didn't believe me when I said you loved Antony. I had to prove it to him." Emilia stands up, rubbing her arm as she walks back behind her desk and takes a seat.

"Is he really injured?"

"He is." Charlie takes the seat next to me. "There was a dirty tackle and he damaged the ligaments in his ankle. He'll be out for the rest of the season. Only problem is, he's refusing to talk to anyone. Feels like he's lost everything—football and you—all in a couple of days. He's wallowing in a world of pain. I needed Shark to make sure what I thought you felt for my friend was genuine because he doesn't deserve to be hurt anymore." He locks his gaze with mine and doesn't look away. Normally I can withstand any amount of scrutiny, but this stare is making me squirm.

"I can't promise that, Charlie. It's why I've held off on making what we were doing official. He wants forever and I don't know if I'm built for that." I look away from him and fiddle with my hands in my lap. I don't know this man and I'm telling him more than I've told the people who are closest to me.

"BULLSHIT!" Emilia shouts. My head shoots up and she smirks. "That's the biggest amount of horse crap I've heard since Nell's 'I don't love William' spiel. You were built for relationships. More than any of us. You love fiercely and take everyone under your sarcastic, sassy, wings. You made Connor a Cooper without hesitation and Verity is yours whether she likes it or not. There's no escape for either of them. You won't let them leave you, ever. You just need to apply your own level of stubbornness to your relationship with Marcello and you'll grow old and grey together like the rest of them."

I shoot daggers at my sister but can't stop the grin that threatens to tip the corners of my mouth. "They couldn't leave even if they wanted to. Connor tried and I shut that shit down." I chuckle.

"So do that with Antony." I shoot daggers at Charlie as he walks over to Emilia. She's smirking, clearly enjoying my discomfort. She's an evil Queen and I love her so damn much.

"The relationship between girlfriend and boyfriend is different, Charlie. What if it doesn't work out between us? I'll be heartbroken and humiliated." I know that my argument sounds weak, but I can't come up with anything else. So I stick with the same bullshit line I've been using forever.

Emilia fixes me with a stare then smiles gently. "And what if it does, Cleo? You could have what Nell and Will have. What Juliet and Connor are building. What Mum and Dad have."

I drop my head, unable to face her uncanny insight. Because I do want all of that. But I'm still bloody scared.

"Did Antony ever tell you about his list? Or what his parents were called?" Charlie asks. I shake my head. He sighs loudly and Emilia cackles in her chair. Charlie looks at her, his eyebrows drawn together and a small smile on his mouth. He's clearly puzzled but carries on with what he was saying.

"When Antony was young he made this list about his ideal woman. When he came and told me he was in love with the party planner—the first day he met you, by the way—he reminded me of everything he wrote. You fit the description perfectly. The cherry on top? You were called Cleopatra, the same as his mum. His dad's Antony senior. What are the odds of that, Cleo? Of meeting someone you described years ago who even has the name you wanted?"

I sit in the chair barely breathing and just blinking at him rapidly. Words unable to form past the emotion clogging my throat.

"Pretty fucking slim, I'd say, Sis," Emilia chimes in. "Do us all a favour and take the bloody risk."

I swallow the lump away and nod my head at them. Charlie hands me a piece of paper with an address and a code written on it.

"Go and see him. He isn't answering anyone's calls. Tell him how you feel and get him out of his pity party. Antony's pretty annoying at the best of times, but when he's miserable and hurting, it's just not normal."

"Odd. You mean 'it's just not odd.' Antony isn't normal. He has his own unique brand of oddness that I fucking love." As the realisation tumbles out of my mouth, adrenaline surges through my veins and I jump up from the chair. "Can you call me a cab?" I ask Emilia as I pull out a compact mirror from my bag. I check that I don't look an absolute mess, thankful I didn't bother with mascara today. As I touch up what little makeup I'm wearing, Emilia turns toward Charlie and holds her hand out to him.

"Give her your car keys." Emilia demands.

He shakes his head, his eyebrows up by his hairline and his eyes frantically darting between me and Emilia. "No way. That car is like my baby. I don't let anyone drive it. Even Zoe. Especially Zoe actually, she can't drive for shit. No, Shark. Absolutely not." Charlie plants his hands firmly on his hips and shakes his head defiantly. Emilia continues to stare him down. He starts to squirm and I know as soon as his eyes flicker from side to side that she's won and he'll give in. My sister's a fucking legend.

"Fine. But if she damages her in any way, you're paying for it, Shark."

Emilia smirks at him. "Deal." He places the fob in her palm and she swivels on her feet tossing them to me.

"Go get your man and bring him back for all of us. He may be annoying, but I am rather fond of his brand of oddness, as you called it."

I laugh as I walk out of her office. My stomach's filled with nerves but my heart's filled with stubbornness. I'm about to take the biggest risk of my life and I just hope Antony is ready for it.

CHAPTER 22

Antony

Shrouded in darkness, I sit in my living room. It matches my mood. My phone has alerted me to various notifications and I've ignored every one of them. I know Charlie has phoned and texted me multiple times, the bridal march ringtone I assigned him telling me so. Baby Shark rang out for Emilia but failed to make me smile like it normally does.

I know the one person I wanted to hear from hasn't bothered. My phone hasn't sung 'Sunflower' by Lenny Kravitz and Drake. She hasn't bothered because she walked away from me. She didn't want what I offered.

I was supposed to be focused on the game and not on her. Fat lot of good that did me. I got fucking injured in the second half. And all I could think of when I was stretchered off the pitch was, *"I wonder if Cleoptara will call me now?"* What an idiot I am. She wasn't in this like I was. She didn't want me the same way I wanted her. All she wanted was to fuck me.

I should've let it happen instead of waiting to make it special. She wanted to date me in secret, and then what? Throw me on the sidelines when she was done. Jeez, I was blinded by her name and my Papa's advice. I should've listened to Charlie and kept our relationship professional.

My silent reverie is over as my phone blares the bridal march song again, but I continue to ignore it. I don't want to speak to Charlie. I've let him and Zoe down and I feel like shit because of it. There's no way I'll be able to finish planning their party with her now. I groan loudly as the ringtone starts again, why does he have to care so much about me?

"What?" I grumble down the phone at him.

"Oh, you finally answered. About fucking time." I roll my eyes even though he can't see me and then frown into the darkness because it reminds me of Cleopatra.

"What do you want, Charlie? I'm really not in the mood."

"Oh I think your mood will be getting a whole lot better in a little bit, Bro." He chuckles and it makes me want to throw my phone against the wall.

"Why? Have you found a cure for fucked up ligaments?" I ask through gritted teeth as he laughs again.

"Come on now, Antony. They're not fucked up. The damage is repairable. Wear the boot, use the crutches, do the physio, and you'll be back to normal in no time." Charlie's reasoning isn't what I want to hear.

"And in the meantime, Brady gets my spot." I growl.

"Until you come back. Coach isn't going to replace you with Brady. If anything this is his chance to prove he can play alongside you and handle life in the big leagues." I run my hand over my head pushing my fingers into my closed eyes.

"Charlie, I need to go. I don't want to deal with all of this now. I'm done. Thanks for checking on me."

"Anytime. Do me a favour though, don't go to bed yet. Stay up for at least an hour. I don't want you sleeping through the day and then annoying me through the night."

I tell him okay and hang the phone up. Silence resumed, I

lean forward and place my elbows on my thighs, cradling my head in my hands. Charlie is right. My ankle injury isn't as bad as it could have been and hopefully Coach welcomes me back into the team when I'm healed. As for Cleopatra, it's over on my part. I'm not chasing anymore. She wanted me to leave her alone, so I will.

I lean back on the sofa and prop my foot back onto the pillows to keep it elevated. I reach for the remote control and freeze as I hear my front door open. Only Charlie and Zoe have the code. I know it's not Charlie as he would've said so when he was on the phone so it must be Zoe checking up on me.

"Zoe, I'm okay. You can leave me alone to wallow despite what Charlie says. I just need a few days to come to terms with the shitshow my life has become." I sigh out loudly as I hear high heeled footsteps glide across my marble floor. The living room door opens and my mouth gapes in shock as I watch Cleopatra stride into the room wearing a black wrapover dress and those red thigh-high boots. What is she doing here? How did she get the code? Why does she have to look so fucking fuckable?

"What do you want, Cleo?" My lust filled voice is gravelly and doesn't sound like my own.

"You, Antony. I want you." She stands in front of me with her arms crossed, forcing her beautiful tits together. Whether she's doing it on purpose or not I don't know, but fuck I want to see them naked. Maybe that's what I should do. If all she wants to do is sleep with me then why should I stop her? She's not in it for love. For forever. She just wants right now? Fine. She can walk out of here when she's done knowing what she's leaving behind.

"You want to fuck me, Cleo? Is that why you're here? Are you pissed off that I never got to explore your body? That you had to imagine what it felt like to have my tongue run over you instead of feeling it? Is that what you want, Cleo? You want me to strip you naked and fuck you all night long?"

I watch her rapid breathing, her eyes black with desire as she licks her lips, clearly enjoying the words coming out of my mouth. I grab my crutches and haul myself off the sofa. Thankfully, I can put a lot of weight on my foot with the boot on so I'm able to stride out of the room and away from her. The idea of fucking her and then watching her walk away causes actual pain in my chest. This isn't me. I'm not the dirty talking, one night stand kind of guy. I don't want to be that guy, but I want her so much I'm willing to be whoever she needs me to be. I hear the click clack of her heels following after me. I turn into my game room and move over to the pool table in the centre of the room. She follows closely behind, stopping just in front of me.

"Yes, I want that, Antony. Of course I do. I've wanted you from the minute I saw you. Who wouldn't?" She places her hands on my shoulders and her touch ignites a fire inside of me. I'm burning from within for this woman who only wants me in this moment. I try to remind myself of this fact, but stop caring as she licks her lips again. I'm instantly filled with a need to taste her all over. Instead I listen as she speaks.

"So many times I've imagined what it would feel like to have your lips on my body. To feel your warm breath on my skin. To taste you. To watch you explode inside of me. Fuck, Antony. You've been the main attraction of my fantasies for a while now. So yeah, I want you." Her eyes are black and there's a pink tint across her cheeks. I lick my lips and watch as her eyes trail across my mouth. Her hands squeeze my shoulders and I smirk as an idea flashes in my mind.

"Prove it." I can see the hesitation in her eyes as she contemplates what I mean. I smirk again. "Prove it to me, Sunflower." The pet name slips from my lips and she moans

146

as I say it. I lean closer, whispering against her ear, "Show me what you did. When you were alone and wishing I was there, touching you, licking you, feeling you."

She closes her eyes at the proximity of our bodies and whispers, "I can't." I let the crutches drop to my sides and I stroke her cheek. She's the reason we're both hurting but I still want to comfort her. My jaw clenches when she takes a deep inhale of breath and bites down on her bottom lip.

"Do you trust me?" I whisper.

She nods her head, her eyes still closed.

"Do as I say then, Cleopatra, and know that when I'm finished with you, none of your fantasies will ever be enough anymore."

I spin around as she opens her eyes and blinks a couple of times. The loss of her touch is like a bucket of cold water has been thrown on me. I quickly limp over to one of the chairs next to the table and signal for her to follow me. Moving a chair so it's in front of me, I motion for her to sit down, then I lean forward, keeping my gaze focused on hers.

"I want you to strip, Sunflower. Everything but the boots." I study her eyes, looking for any kind of hesitation, but all I can see is desire. The need for us.

She stands slowly and unties the bow at the side of her dress, unwrapping herself for me. Saliva pools in my mouth, I'm literally drooling for this woman. She peels the dress from her body and keeps her eyes burning into mine. Once the dress is gone completely I sit back and admire her. She's fucking gorgeous. Her skin is like porcelain with a pink tinge over her cheeks and neck, brushing over her lace covered breasts. She stands before me looking like a goddess dressed in red. My eyes take their fill, committing every detail to memory in case this is the first and last time I'll ever get to see her like this.

She shifts on her feet and I bring my eyes back to hers. As

147

soon as they lock together, her nervous squirm disappears and her mouth parts as she reads the approval on my face.

"Take your bra and thong off too, Sunflower." She nods, unclipping her bra from the front and I watch in awe as her breasts spring free. I take a deep breath and stand. Her eyes are so dark they're black as she takes a step closer to me.

"Stop! You do as I say, Cleopatra, or this stops now."

She goes to speak but nods again instead.

I lift my t-shirt off and smirk as her eyes greedily trail over my body. I lower my shorts and thank God they're big enough to get over the boot. She zeros her attention to my covered dick and licks her lips again. I hook my thumbs into the sides of my boxers and wait for her to do the same. She lowers the lace, baring her beautiful pussy. My dick surges up and I fist it hard to try to relieve some of the ache her naked body is causing. She moans loudly and watches my fist wrap around it. I chuckle and sit back down.

"Sit down, Cleopatra." She sits and crosses her legs. "Nuh-uh. Open up and let me see your pussy, Sunflower."

Her breathing is so rapid that I'm slightly worried she's going to pass out. She opens her legs and I can see her glistening with her arousal. Her scent floats through the room and my mouth waters again at what she'll taste like.

"Touch yourself, Cleopatra. Imagine it's me sliding my hand down your throat and cupping your breast. Rolling your nipple in between my fingers until you're moaning in ecstasy. I want to hear you, Sunflower."

She follows my instructions, the pink tint turning red as she does. It travels down her body like her hand and spreads over her chest. She palms her breast moaning as her fingers pluck her nipple. She cries out my name. Hearing it leave her lips and seeing her beautiful body like this is enough to tip me over the edge. My balls are aching and pre cum leaks from my tip. I squeeze my hand around my dick, moving up and down, slowly, because I don't want to come until I'm inside her.

"With your other hand, slowly reach down and stroke your pussy. Go nice and slow. Drive yourself crazy." She does as I say and her hand trails down her body. Her fingers glide through her silky folds and are quickly slicked with arousal. Her moans and groans are driving me wild. She's a picture of perfection. Her hands on her body and those fucking red, thigh-high boots.

Shit. I fist myself harder. Imagining it's her hand wrapped around me.

"Make sure you don't come, Cleopatra. I want you coming on my dick, not on your fingers." She opens her eyes, our gazes locking together. She flicks her eyes down and moans as she watches my hand glide up and down.

"Antony." She whines and it's the last straw.

I growl, "Get up, Sunflower." She stands quickly.

"Bend over the pool table. I want to fuck you whilst you're wearing those boots." She whimpers and moves quickly to the table. She drapes her body over it and waves her pert little arse for me. I walk over to the cabinet near the table and grab some condoms. I rip one open with my teeth, placing it on my throbbing dick, and ask her, "Do you still want me, Cleopatra?"

"Fuck yes, Antony. I want the forever kind with you."

I can't think too much about what that means because my dick is seeking her heat. I stride over to her, admiring her beautiful arse as I do. I stroke my hand over the round cheeks. I let my hand caress her spine. Featherlight strokes. Her hips sway, trying to get any kind of friction to her pussy. With each sway she brushes her arse on my dick. Groaning at the contact, I place it at her entrance. I slide it up and down her slit, covering it in her juices.

"God, Antony. Please. Take me. I'm yours," she moans out to me.

I let a groan rumble from my chest as I bury myself in her. She cries out as our bodies finally become one. I can't feel anything apart from Cleopatra. Her pussy grips onto me, her muscles clinging to me. She's so tight and wet that I know I'm not going to last long.

"Cleopatra, fuck. You feel so good, Baby. So good." I tell her on each thrust as she cries out in pleasure.

"Antony. Yes! Antony! Fuck! I'm coming. Antony, I'm coming." She screams my name once more and I can feel her clench around my dick. The tingle starts at the base of my spine and I know I'm not going to hold off any longer. I thrust into her. Once. Twice more. And I explode inside her shouting, "My Sunflower."

CHAPTER 23

Cleo

Tingles shoot through my naked body from the most intense orgasm anyone has ever given me. Antony's laying on top of me. The weight of him is comforting. His hands are splayed on the table, on either side of my head, and I manoeuvre one of my hands so that it's resting on top of his. When I tangle our fingers together, he pulls away. He lifts himself off me and the lack of his warmth causes shivers to wrack through my body.

His footsteps thud behind me and I remember his injury and spring into action. "Shit, Antony. Your foot. Where are your crutches?" I duck down and pick them up, walking over to him. Waiting as he discards the condom in the bin, I hand him the crutches and he mumbles, "thanks" as he hobbles off to the other side of the room, grabbing his shorts as he goes.

"You don't have to stay, Cleo. You can go now. You got what you wanted from me. What you've always wanted from me."

He looks so sad. There's no twinkle in his eyes, the fire is merely a flicker. Gone is the dominant man who just ruined me for any other guy. He puts his shorts on as I walk over to him. I grab his biceps, digging my fingers in tightly, forcing him to pay attention to what I'm about to say.

"Antony, I came here to tell you something. Not to fuck you. I didn't get a chance to because…" I take a deep breath and smile at him.

"I want the forever kind, Antony. I want to try it with you. I want to tell my family we're dating. That I'm your girl-friend. I want you to annoy me with your incessant texts again. I want to meet your mum and dad. I want to be yours. I want you to be mine. And I'm not taking no for an answer." I hold my breath and sigh in relief as a grin overtakes the sullen look on his face. "You were right. I've come to love your brand of oddness, Antony. I love you." I lower my eyes so he can't see the vulnerability in them, but he raises my chin and forces me to look at him.

"For real?" He locks his gaze with mine and I nod. "Why didn't you tell me that before? I'm so sorry."

I frown at him. "Why are you sorry?"

The look on his face is so conflicted, but so raw and honest. His voice is part guilt part contrition as he tells me, "I wouldn't have fucked you like that. I would've made love to you, Cleopatra."

I'm stunned. I blink at him, and his confusion at my reac-tion likely matches my confusion from moments ago. I can't help my smile as I blurt, "Are you kidding? That was THE hottest thing I've ever experienced in my life. I thoroughly enjoyed being fucked by you, Antony. I would also like to experience you making love to me. But I understand if you need time to get there again. To believe and trust what I say and who I am enough to love me. There's no rush. I'm not going anywhere this time." I try to make my words sound convincing but I hear the nerves and fear in my voice. And I know he does too.

He looks at me and smirks. "Sunflower, I've loved you

from the minute I saw you. That hasn't changed because you needed more time to figure it out. This is real, isn't it? This isn't a fever dream? You're actually standing here in nothing but red thigh high boots and you're declaring your love for me."

I laugh at the absurdity of everything. "Yes, it's real. Very fucking real, Antony." I take a breath and force myself to hold his gaze. "I'm sorry I hurt you. I'm sorry I was too scared to tell everyone we were together even though I think they all knew anyway. I'm sorry…"

He drops his crutches to the floor and places his hand over my mouth to stop my apologies. "Enough. It's okay, Sunflower. You're here and you love me and that's all that matters now. How did you get in though?"

I giggle under his palm and mumble, "Charlie."

"That's why he told me not to go to bed and said my mood would be getting better soon. Fucker." He chuckles and wraps his arms around me. I sigh into him, feeling content and scared but happy too.

"I didn't see what happened at the game. I was hiding in my office after pretending to go out all night for the past couple of days. I didn't want to have to answer Juliet's questions about us. Emilia summoned me to her office and Charlie was there."

He chuckles, "Charlie teamed up with Shark?"

I nod my head that's buried in his bare chest. "Yep. Charlie didn't believe Emilia when she said I loved you. He needed proof. So she made out you were injured worse than you were. It broke my defences down and made me think I'd lost you for real." I grip him tighter as the panic I felt at the idea of losing him flashes through my head. "Charlie gave me the code to your house and your address. And then Emilia forced him to let me use his car to get here."

"Holy shit. No way. He gave you the keys to Stella?"

I lift my head at his shocked words and grin at his slack jaw and eyes so wide they look like they'll pop out of his head. "Yep. She made him. I think it's hilarious you're all so scared of her."

His chest vibrates with his laughter. "Shark is scary. She also controls a huge part of our careers and lives. If she wanted to, she could screw us over big time. Good job, I'm basically her brother-in-law now." He grins mischievously and I roll my eyes.

"One step at a time, Marcello." He kisses the top of my head as I lay my cheek back against his chest, and I shiver with excitement at knowing this man wants to marry me.

Taking my shiver as a sign that I'm cold, Antony grips me tightly and I feel his dick stirring against my bare skin. "Sorry, Sunflower. Let's go to bed and warm up."

I smile up at him, "Okay, but you have to use your crutches to walk, Antony. I don't want to be the reason for your injury to get worse."

"Deal. Besides I think you've got some making up to do to me anyway, so my ankle will get plenty of rest whilst I'm laying down." He grins and winks.

"Well come on, Stallion. It's time for my ride. Yee haw!" I holler and strut out of the game room, exaggerating the sway in my hips for his benefit. I hear him growl after me and then snicker as I come to an abrupt stop. We both realise I have no idea where his bedroom is and I'm standing naked, apart from my boots, in a huge foyer. I'm looking around in awe at just how big and beautiful this house is when Antony steps up behind me.

"It's a breathtaking sight, isn't it?"

"It's a beautiful house, Antony." I turn my head to find him staring at my arse.

"I wasn't talking about the house, Sunflower." He slaps my buttcheek and I jump.

I spin to face him with my teeth digging into my bottom lip. The sting of his palm on my arse causes me to squeeze my thighs together to stop the ache in my pussy. His eyes catch the movement and darken with lust.

"Upstairs now, Cleopatra," he growls out.

I don't hesitate this time and I scoot up the huge staircase, turning around at the top to watch Antony stalk after me. This was definitely the right choice to make.

CHAPTER 24

Cooper Clans Curiosity - group texts

Emilia: Cleopatra? Can we have a text letting us know what the state of play is please? We've given you ample time…

Marcus: I love it when she gets all professional. My boo (Red heart emoji)

Emilia: (Red heart emoji)

Nell: Damn, emojis. Is this a state of play on what I think it is?

Emilia: Yep.

Juliet: OMG

Nell: Seriously? I'm running on no sleep and can text in full words and sentences and you can't even write, 'Oh my God,' Juliet?

Juliet: (Eyeroll emoji) FML, FON

Nell: I have no idea what those acronyms mean…

Cleo: FUCK MY LIFE, and at a guess, FUCK OFF NELL. Am I right, Princess?

Juliet: YES! That's why I love you the most, Cleo.

Nell: Brats!

Emilia: So…

Antony: We're practically related, Shark (winking emoji)

Emilia: *Sigh* I'm annoyed by that knowledge and also

happy about it. Even through text messages you manage to annoy me, Marcello.

Cleo: I know that feeling.

Antony: You weren't calling me annoying last night, Sunflower.

Marcus: Yes! Get it, Cleo. Antony, my man!

Cleo: (Eyeroll emoji)

Marcus: Is that your eyes rolling because of the D you got last night?

Connor: Too far, Bro.

Will: Marcus…

Cleo: (Laughing emoji)

Antony: (Eggplant emoji, laughing emoji, eyeroll emoji)

Will: Oh. My. God. There are two of them. Cleo, what have you done?

Juliet: Antony, apparently (Monkey hiding his mouth emoji)

Cleo: I did. More than once. (Winking emoji)

Emilia: And I think I'm going to vomit. I may have to leave my own family's group chat. Marcello, this is your fault.

Antony: Nu-uh. Marcus brought it up.

Marcus: Is that your way of saying you were thinking of me when you were playing hide the salami with Cleo?

Antony: ERM…

Cleo: Definitely wasn't you he was thinking about, Bitch.

Marcus: Oh kitty has claws when it comes to her man. I like it, Cleo baby.

Marcus: Am I okay to call her baby, Antony? Last time I called a Cooper woman baby I got growled at, eh Tiger…

Connor: FOM

Juliet: (Laughing hysterically emoji)

Nell: I'm so happy for you, Cleo. You too, Antony. Fancy babysitting your new niece so I can sleep? Just kidding. But not really kidding…

Antony: Anytime. Cleo and I will be more than happy to help.

Cleo: We will?

Antony: Sunflower, your sister needs help.

Cleo: Fine. You're on nappy duty though, I'll be with Ben.

Antony: Deal.

Nell: Are you serious?

Cleo: Looks like it.

CHAPTER 25
Antony

It's Saturday night and Cleopatra and I have spent the past week at my house 'getting to know each other.' Tonight all frisky business has to be put aside as we prepare for a night of babysitting duties. I love babies and kids. I'm always the first one to sign up for the kid days at the club, and I truly love spending time with them. Ben was the coolest little dude when we went fake trick or treating. He's funny, clever and as sarcastic as his auntie. I can't wait for Cleo to get back from picking them up.

I would've gone with her but I wanted to make sure the house was safe enough for them even though Cleo already said it was. In fact I think her exact words were, "Twatface, stop. Bea can't even roll over yet so don't worry about not having the plug sockets covered." I chuckle as I remember the eyeroll that followed and the smack on her arse that came next. I try not to focus on what happened after that as I'm trying to keep my dick in check and picturing Cleopatra's naked body, riding me like a cowgirl, isn't going to help.

"We're back." The front door slams behind them and a wail comes from the carseat Cleopatra's lugging into the foyer.

Ben sheepishly looks at me and grimaces, "Sorry."

I limp over to them and ruffle his hair. "Don't sweat it, Benny boy. I'll make her happy again." He smiles up at me as Cleopatra walks past us into the living room.

She places the carseat on my coffee table and blows out a frazzled breath. "Right I'll go back to the car and get the rest of their stuff. Babies need a shitload of crap." She shakes her head as she turns on her heel and walks out.

Ben tuts at her as she does. "She needs to put money in da jar."

I chuckle at him and place my crutches on the floor before I unclip Bea and lift her into my arms. I shush her and sit on the sofa as Ben grabs his tablet from his little suitcase on wheels and sits next to us.

"Can I watch this for a bit?" he asks, almost reluctantly. I nod and he pumps his little fist in triumph snuggling into my sofa with his headphones on.

Bea is still grumbling so I place her on my chest and pat her tiny bum gently. "You're okay, baby girl. I'll look after you. Your big bro's here and your beautiful Auntie Cleopatra too. You're in safe hands, I promise." I rock her gently and turn my head when I hear a gasp in the doorway. Cleopatra is holding a bag in each hand and staring at me.

"You okay, Sunflower?"

A heated look flashes across her face and she drops the bags and strides toward me. She stands in front of my knees, bends down and kisses me. Her mouth is hard and moves fast on my lips. "There is nothing sexier than a man cradling a tiny baby, and I never thought I'd think that. You're doing all kinds of things to me, Antony."

My cheeks hurt from smiling so much. This is the Cleopatra I always knew was in there somewhere. The one I truly crave.

Cleo straightens up and snaps Ben's headphones and he frowns up at her. "Ow, Auntie Cleo."

She grins, her hands going to her hips. "I want to show you where you're sleeping tonight. We can put your bags in there and then I can show you the games room."

I smirk at the blush that stains her cheeks at the mention of that room. She sticks her tongue out at me and a laugh rumbles through my chest, jostling baby Bea awake. I murmur, "shit," under my breath.

"I heard dat Uncle Antony. You need to put money in da jar." He grins and I'm caught out by the emotion that rises in me hearing uncle attached to my name. My gaze meets Cleopatra's and she gives me a smile and a wink.

"Come on, Benvolio. Let's warm Bea's bottle up and *Uncle* Antony can feed your sister whilst we explore this huge house." She holds out her hand to Ben who takes hold of it and I mouth, "thank you." I needed the time to gather myself. That little dude has accepted me straight into his heart.

Happiness overwhelms me as I lower the perfect pink bundle from my chest, laying her on my thighs. I rock her gently, telling her, "Your brother called me Uncle Antony. You can too. I promise I'll always be here for you both."

Cleopatra walks back into the room, places a cloth under Bea's chin, and hands me the bottle. She kisses me on my cheek and struts out with Ben as I tell his sister, "Come on, Sweetheart. Let's eat."

~

"Please," I beg Cleopatra.

"Nope." She shakes her head at me and Ben grins at the pair of us.

"I'll buy you anything you want," I offer her.

"Nope." She pops the P and crosses her arms over her chest.

"How about you, Ben? Want to help your uncle out?" I smile down and watch as he copies his auntie's stance, shaking his head.

"Sorry Unc, I'm too little." He smirks up at me and Cleo cackles in amusement.

"Fine. I'll do it myself." I look down at Bea in her travel cot and grimace at the state of her. Her cute little pale pink all in one suit is covered in yellow foul smelling goo. I gingerly lift her out and hold her at arm's length. I walk over to the table that I've turned into a makeshift changing station and place her down on the mat.

"Jeez, Bea. How did you turn milk into this, Girl?" I gag a little as I unbutton the millions of poppers on her suit, shooting eye daggers at Ben and Cleopatra as they laugh in the doorway. "You could help instead of laughing, you know. Why are you Coopers so mean?" This just makes them laugh more. My focus is lost, my hand slips, and now I'm covered in baby poop.

"For fu- fudge sake!" I lift my hand for them to see, which of course causes even more laughing.

"Stop, I need to pee!" comes from the littlest laugh as he runs off in the direction of the nearest bathroom.

"Sunflower," I plead.

Finally taking pity on me, although still giggling, she grabs the wipes and cleans my hand. "You're such a twat," is whispered right before she places a kiss on the tip of my nose.

I manage to get the baby cleaned and into new clothes as Cleopatra deals with the poopy clothes and wipes down the travel cot. Ben sits on the sofa next to me and I place Bea in his arms with a pillow propped under them. Cleo walks in and freezes, staring at us for a second before lifting her phone to take a picture. She sits on Ben's other side and turns the camera on selfie mode. As we grin at the screen, I think to myself I want a copy of that one. I watch in amazement as she puts it as her home screen. She turns to look at me, raises her eyebrow, and tilts her head. Instead of saying anything, I smile and wink. I silently pray that in a few years, I'll be doing exactly this but with our own kids here as well.

CHAPTER 26

Birthdays with the Coopers – group texts

Marcus: My birthday is less than three weeks away, people. Did everyone get my gift list?

Connor: I didn't.

Cleo: I lost it, sorry.

Will: NO.

Juliet: Ummm.

Nell: Nu-uh.

Antony: Don't know what you're talking about.

Emilia: NOPE.

Marcus: You lot suck.

Marcus: Boo, you hurt me the most.

Emilia: I'm sorry but your list is ridiculous.

Marcus: What's so ridiculous about it?

Juliet: For one, Connor is NOT dressing up as Thor for you.

Cleo: And Antony isn't reenacting certain scenes from films for you, no matter how much he looks like either actor… he saves those skills for me (winking emoji)

Nell: And we will not reconsider and add your name as a middle name for Bea or Ben, so just drop it.

Marcus: Well it's nice to know where I stand with you all.

Emilia: Antony isn't it your birthday in a few weeks too?

Antony: It is but it's no big deal. I don't have a list like some people…

Marcus: More fool you.

Marcus: When's your birthday?

Will: May Second.

Antony: Erm, yeah May second…

Marcus: WTD Will?

Cleo: Stalker alert.

Will: It was in his stats and it stuck in my head I don't know why.

Marcus: Maybe because it's the same ducking birthday as your best friend!

Marcus: Dick!

Antony: No way. We have the same birthday?

Marcus: Birthday twins, Baby.

Marcus: No need to growl now, tiger.

Connor: FOM

Marcus: Should we throw a party?

Cleo: NO!

Juliet: NO!

Connor: NO!

Emilia: NO!

Will: NO!

Marcus: Jeez, Antony, they do not want to celebrate you, Bro.

Cleo: It's not that, you dick. We've got so much still to do for the engagement party…

Juliet: We just had Connor's…

Nell: Why don't we just have a nice dinner together or something?

Marcus: Okay, okay no party. But seeing as I'm being so reasonable, Emilia, there was something on my list you could give me that wasn't ridiculous…

Emilia: There really wasn't.

Marcus: Boo. There were two actually. A list of all the single clients' numbers so I can find myself an HEA. And letting me go to the ball with you… PRETTY PLEASE?

Antony: I can get you their numbers as long as I don't have to reenact certain scenes for you…

Emilia: Stop encouraging him, Marcello. And don't even think about giving him Lockheart's number.

Antony: You spoil all my fun, Shark.

Cleo: What ball?

Juliet: What ball?

Nell: What ball?

Cleo: (Laughing emoji)

Juliet: (Laughing emoji)

Emilia: (Eyeroll emoji)

Nell: Laughing out loud, guys.

Juliet: Seriously Nell?

Cleo: (Eyeroll emoji) just type LOL you loser.

Marcus: *Cough, focus on the ball, Cough*

Emilia: Thanks, Boo (Swearing emoji)

Marcus: I needed reinforcements, so I called in the cavalry.

Emilia: I'm not going so I can't take you with me, Marcus.

Nell: WHAT BALL?

Cleo: Nell's shouting, tell us what ball before she starts speaking in emojis.

Nell: I'm close, Cleo. Very fucking close to sending those annoying little faces to Emilia.

Juliet: Oh lord, Em, just tell us.

Emilia: It's times like this I wish I were an only child…

Emilia: My boss is retiring and is throwing an elaborate masquerade ball as his retirement party.

Emilia: It's ridiculously pretentious. Absurdly expensive. And will be filled with a bunch of men who think they can drool and fawn over the women that attend. Even the ones who make more money, have a better client list and will kick their fucking arses.

Nell: Are you in danger of losing your job?

Emilia: No. He's handing the reins over to his son who lives in America. He's relocating to live here. Probably has little to no knowledge on sport over here and if I hear him say 'soccer' once, I may maim him.

Juliet: But won't it look bad if you don't attend?

Marcus: Yes, it will look soooo bad. That's why you should attend with a smoking hot man on your arm.

Antony: Aw thanks Marcus, but I think it would be weird if she turned up with me seeing as I'm a client...

Cleo: and dating her sister (angry emoji)

Antony: Oops that too

Marcus: Funny, Twatface. You know I wasn't talking about you.

Connor: I don't think I should go either.

Marcus: (Angry face emoji, middle finger emoji)

Marcus: Boo, please?

Emilia: (Eyeroll emoji) if I agree will you leave me alone?

Marcus: About this? Yes. In general? No, I love you too much to leave you alone.

Emilia: Damn, Marcus. Call me your fairy godmother, looks like we're off to the ball.

Marcus: YAY. I ducking love you, boo.

Marcus: You're still getting me an actual present though, right?

Marcus: Emilia?

Marcus: Boo?

Marcus: You can run but you can't hide...

CHAPTER 27

Cleo

"Emilia, I'm screwed." I whisper-shout into the phone as I leave another department store empty handed. "What the actual fuck am I supposed to get the man who can afford everything? Apart from giving him myself naked wrapped in a red bow, I have no idea." As I dodge around people walking everywhere in a hurry, I hear Emilia gag a little on the other end of the line. But my frustration is so bad, I'm unable to take any pleasure from nauseating my big sister.

"That's an image I'll have in my head forever now. Thank you, Brat. You're looking at this all wrong, Cleo. What does Antony love more than anything?" I head into another store and instantly feel like Julia Roberts in *Pretty Woman* when the sales clerk eyes up my all black ensemble with yellow doc martin boots. As I roll my eyes at her obvious look of disdain, she shakes her head and takes a step closer. I haven't got time for her snooty self, so I pointedly ignore her instead of giving her what for and casually browse the hangers, looking at blah top after blah top.

"I don't know, Emilia. You seem to know him a lot better than I do, so why don't you just tell me." I don't mean to snap at my sister but I'm pissed off. Pissed that the stupid sales woman is being a bitch for no reason. Pissed that I didn't know it was Antony's birthday but my sister did. Just like I don't know what to get him but she seems to.

I'm probably the worst gift giver in the family as well— I'm notorious for giving people hugs instead of presents as I'm shit at them. I always get something they either have, don't like, or don't want. I have the greatest of intentions but I can never get it right, and right now it feels like it's imperative that I get it right. I've put a ridiculous amount of pressure on this present and I'm running out of time. I only have two days left.

"Cleo, you're spiralling and nothing good ever comes from that. Where are you now? What shop?" I look around, trying to see the name of the shop I'm in but must look suspicious or something as little Miss Snooty-pants comes marching over.

"Erm, Miss," her lips twist in distaste as she speaks and I want to throat punch her, but I don't. "I don't think we have anything *you* can afford in here. Maybe the charity shop around the corner can help," she says with a smirk on her face, but I turn my scowl on her and it drops away.

"Listen lady, I am a successful business owner. I run a high end events management company and I can afford whatever the fuck I want to in this grotesque little hellhole you call a shop. Your clothes are tatty and poor quality, yet nothing about their price tag is as off putting as your presence here." As the lady starts to protest, I hold my hand in her face and she flinches back. "I have a lot of shopping to do and a lot of money to spend on my very talented, exceptionally handsome boyfriend's birthday and I really don't have time for petty little mean girls who still act like they're in high school, looking down on anyone who dares to be themselves instead of a clone of what they think they should be. I have to go shopping now." I say as I head out of the shop, Emilia's laughter ringing in my ear.

"Cleopatra Cooper, you little badass! I fucking love you. You Pretty Woman'd her. That was epic. Leave Marcello's gift to me. I know exactly what to send him from you. Trust me." Before I can agree, she's hung up. And I don't have the heart to call her back and tell her no. That I actually wanted to be the one to figure out what to get him. Even though I still have no bloody idea, and that notion is causing the anxiety I've managed to keep at bay to build up until it's sitting in the pit of my stomach. I'm not cut out for this.

CHAPTER 28

Antony

"Happy Birthday, Antony!" the Cooper clan cheers as I walk through the door. My boot causes a loud thud as I step over the threshold and they all glance down at it, working hard not to change their excitement to pity grins. Fortunately, it's not just my birthday, and the other celebrant is happy as always to draw their attention.

"And what am I? A ducking ghost or something? You lot are a joke. Someone new and shiny comes in and you fawn all over them." Marcus folds his arms over his chest and pouts so I step next to him and wrap my arm around his shoulder.

"Happy Birthday, Twin." He grins and throws his arms around me, making me wobble a little. The look of near panic on his face is adorable, but he steadies me and grins as he says sorry.

"We didn't forget you Marcus. Happy Birthday," Juliet tells him and steps forward to give him a hug.

As Marcus holds her tightly he puts his nose into her hair and sniffs loudly. I swear I hear Connor growl from the corner.

"Ha! I told you, Princess. Is this shirt apt or what?"

Marcus opens his jacket and shows us all the black t-shirt he's wearing with 'GRRRRRRRR' written across it in purple writing. Juliet bursts into laughter, as do Nell and Emilia. Will smirks and Connor frowns at him whilst I stand completely perplexed, but absolutely entertained by it all.

～

"Dinner was delicious, Connor, thank you." I extend the compliment as I lean back in my chair, a little fuller than I probably should be considering I can't just work all the extra off on the pitch. The rest of the Coopers murmur their agreements and Connor dips his head in gratitude.

"Please tell me it's time for presents now. I've been grown up enough. I want my presents. I'm not opposed to throwing a tantrum, you know. Full on throwing myself on the floor, kicking and crying. The works."

"He's not lying. It's how he got me to agree to live with him," Connor tells me and Marcus splutters into his drink.

"I think it was you who begged me to move in with you, Not Hemsworth, not the other way around," Marcus retorts as Connor chuckles quietly at him.

"Oh for God's sake, stop bitching, the pair of you. Let's go into the living room and clean up later. I want to see how much you like my gift, Boo." We all follow suit as Emilia stands up and heads into the living room.

I sit down on the sofa and when Cleopatra sits next to me, I wrap my arm around her shoulder and bring her closer. She rests her head on my shoulder and I smile in contentment, not needing anything more for my birthday than I already have. As Marcus starts to unwrap his gifts, I kiss Cleopatra's head.

"Are you for real? Boo! This is amazing." Marcus throws himself at Emilia and she laughs as she catches him, but as

172

she's sitting on the foot stool, she falls backward with him landing on top of her.

"What is it?" Nell shouts over at them and Marcus pops his head up, looking like a meerkat.

"A designer watch. I'm… I… I…"

"Wow, if I'd known that would make him speechless I'd have gotten him one years ago," Will says and Marcus flips him the bird.

Connor thrusts his gift at him and smirks as he says, "Happy Birthday."

"Thanks, Tiger," Marcus replies and rips open the wrapping to find a frame with a picture of Connor dressed as Thor. "Oh, Not Hemsworth, you gave me you as Thor. I'll treasure it." Connor grins and Cleopatra giggles next to me.

Will picks up more presents, throwing me a little gift. It feels soft and squishy. A quick glance at the label reveals it's from Cleopatra. I open it to find a pair of sunflower socks and chuckle at the sight of them. "To match the ones you got me," she tells me gently. I kiss her forehead, bend down and put one of the socks on my good foot, and wiggle my toes at her. Then I reach over and bring her foot up and into my lap and place the other sock on her opposite foot. "Now we have a matching pair, Sunflower." She rolls her eyes but smiles and leans into me and I kiss the top of her head.

Will hands another present to me and I frown when I see it. "This is for me?" I ask the room and Cleopatra nods her head.

"I suck at finding gifts for people, so Emilia helped me pick something else for you." She looks over and smiles at Emilia who gives her a wink back. "Open it. I hope you like it."

I frown when I hear the shyness in her voice as she encourages me to open it. Unwrapping the paper carefully, my curiosity takes over when I start to see the edges of a frame. "I hope this isn't Connor dressed as Thor because I won't be as happy as Marcus was," I tell them and revel in their laughter. I pull the paper off faster now and stop short at the image in my hand. My eyes scan the beautiful painting of a sunflower and I'm just about to say thank you when I catch the name at the bottom: Cleopatra Cooper.

Turning my stunned eyes toward her, I ask, "Did you paint this?"

She nods, biting on her bottom lip nervously. I reach out and release her lip, running my thumb over the abused flesh. "It's amazing. It'll take pride of place in my house. Thank you for giving me this, Cleopatra."

A smile changes her face from nervous to elated and she hugs me tightly. As we let go, she looks at Emilia and mouths, 'thank you.' These Cooper sisters are always there for each other, no matter what, and I'm so glad they've taken me into their clan. I just hope that when I ask to make it official, my sunflower says yes.

CHAPTER 29

Antony

That was the best birthday ever. After presents were opened, the clan informed Marcus that they weren't going to let our birthdays slide by without a party. Mr and Mrs Cooper came and collected the kids, we cleaned the dishes away, Nell and Will broke out the alcohol and turned the music up. A house party with most of my favourite people in the world was not a shabby way to celebrate my birthday at all. I was a little disappointed Charlie and the team couldn't be here to celebrate with me but they have important matches to prepare for.

We partied well into the early hours and then crashed at Nell's house. Connor and Juliet took Bea's room and we snagged Ben's. He has a small double bed so we were still able to sleep side by side. The only problem is it's five am and I'm wide awake and Cleo already warned me not to wake her up before ten. Turns out, she's exceptionally grumpy in the morning—unless I wake her up with my head between her thighs. But I can't do that in Ben's bed and with her sisters down the hall.

Instead, I tiptoe out of the room—which is extremely hard to do with a boot on your foot, but at least I was allowed to ditch the crutches—and head down to the kitchen. I'm shocked when I see the light on and the door slightly ajar. Knock quietly first so I don't startle or disturb anyone, I slowly open the door, giving whoever is inside enough time to tell me to get lost if they want. As the door opens, I grin when I see Shark sitting at the table, nursing a cup of tea.

She rolls her eyes at me and grins back. "How did I know it'd be you, Marcello?"

I shrug my shoulders at her. "Lucky guess?"

She motions to the kettle with her head, "Want a cup of tea or are you a coffee drinker like Cleo?" She goes to stand and I place my hand on her shoulder to stop her.

"Sit down and enjoy your tea in peace. I'm sure I can find my way around in here." I flip the switch and manage to find the mugs and coffee. "This layout is similar to Cleopatra's." I turn and lean against the counter and watch as Emilia smiles at me. She looks younger, no makeup on and with no work stress to deal with. Being here with her family suits her.

"All of our kitchens are similar layouts to Mum's. I suppose it makes us feel like we're at home in our own houses. Does that make sense?" She scrunches her nose up and I chuckle.

"It does. I like this side of you, Shark. I understand why you have to be such a badass at work, and I thank you for it. You've made me a shitload of money over the years. But this side, it's special. Thank you for letting me see it."

She lowers her eyes from me, shielding me from seeing her vulnerability. I turn back around to give her a moment and finish making my coffee.

"Thank you, Marcello. Not just for saying that, but for making my sister happy. She deserves all the happiness in the world and I know you're the man to give her it."

I take a seat opposite her and place my elbows on the

table. "If I tell you a secret, you won't tell Cleopatra? Or Marcus?"

She grins at me. "I'm not known as the best Cooper secret keeper for nothing, you know."

I blow out a breath. "I want to ask her to marry me. I'm going to look for a ring. Want to help me?"

I watch as a huge grin takes over her face and she grabs my hand and holds it tightly. "Fuck, yes. I mean, I'm not thrilled you'll be my brother-in-law and I'll be stuck with you at work and in the family, but I'm so happy for you both."

I can see the happiness in her eyes but I also note the sadness too. I want to ask about it, but it's not my place. Instead I grin mischievously. "Let's just drop the in-law business. I'll be your brother, Shark."

Her eyes fill with gratitude that I've skipped over her emotions and her mouth tips up at the edges slightly. "Let's not."

Footsteps approach in the hall and Emilia snatches her hand away from mine and schools her face into her usual nonchalant look. I lean back in my chair and bring the coffee to my lips as my sunflower walks in and grunts at us both.

"Coffee."

Emilia chuckles, clearly used to her sister's morning grumbles, and flips the switch on the kettle. Cleo attempts to sit on Emilia's vacated chair but I swipe her off her feet and plonk her on my lap. She snuggles into me, fitting perfectly. I love her like this. She's too sleepy to moan about my pda and forgets that she's supposed to be the Queen of Darkness. I kiss the top of her head, inhaling her scent at the same time.

Happiness engulfs me. It's the best birthday I've ever had. The best gift is snuggled on my lap and will hopefully be wearing my ring in the next few weeks. Everything is perfect.

CHAPTER 30

Antony

The adrenaline rush that normally happens toward the end of the season is lacking for me. Normally I'm up to my eyeballs in training, matches, and worrying about who's topping the league. This year, I'm sidelined and focused on physio.

It's different. My life is at a point where I'm genuinely happy, and football isn't the catalyst for that. I'm ecstatic with the team. They're smashing it, having only lost a handful of games since I've been out. We're up there with the best of the best, and even though I've been injured, I'm still a part of that. I'm so proud of how far we've come.

I'm not happy Brady is still making so many headlines after he told me he wouldn't, but I can't do anything about that. Charlie's already had words and so has Emilia, even though he isn't officially her client yet. I'm hoping she takes him under her wing and straightens him out. He needs guidance from the right people, not the buffoon he currently calls his agent.

Everything is in place for Charlie and Zoe's engagement party—the party that will ruin all engagement parties in the future. Their prom style event will be fucking epic. The perfect party to celebrate Charlie and Zoe's love, and a chance for the boys to let off steam after their season's finished. Cleopatra has worked her cute little arse off to make everything perfect for my best friends, and I couldn't love her more for it if I tried.

Thinking of Cleopatra's arse has my dick twitching in my pants and a smirk forming on my lips. Images of her bent over my pool table, wearing nothing but those sexy as sin, red thigh-highs flash in my head. The urge to reach down and fist my dick is strong. I need to give it some relief as it pushes against the zipper of my jeans, but I can't. Instead I shift on my seat to try to relieve the throb. I swipe all thoughts of Cleopatra and her boots out of my mind and refocus on my plan of action for today.

I'm meeting Shark, Charlie and Zoe for lunch and then we're off to look for engagement rings. I've booked an appointment with the best jeweller in Hatton Garden and everyone's agreed to keep it top secret. I don't want any hints of this getting out in the press. The last thing any of us need is Cleopatra being hounded by paparazzi. I know Charlie has some reservations about how quickly I'm moving, but I also know he'll support me no matter what. He's worried she isn't ready for this, but I know she is. Even if she thinks she isn't, I know she was meant for me. I felt it the first time I saw her. She was made for me and I for her.

I spot Shark walking into the restaurant and notice the scowl on her face before I see the phone glued to her ear. I feel sorry for the person on the other end. Emilia's wrath is something no one wants to be on the receiving end of. She strides toward the table and I catch the end of her conversation.

"No, Marcus. You're being ridiculous." Her tone is sharp and I've never heard her call him by his name before, it's always Boo.

"I don't care what he looks like. I don't care how much

money he has. I do not want a blind date with anyone. Now drop it." She stabs her finger on the screen to hang up and throws the phone into her bag.

She catches the waiter's attention and before he's made it to our table she's asked, "Can I get a large house wine, please?" He scurries off in the other direction as she breathes out a sigh and drops onto the chair opposite me.

"Tough day?" I ask.

She shoots me a death stare as I grin back. "Marcus is being a fucking imbecile and has it in his head that I need to find my happily ever after now that I'm the last Cooper sister left on the shelf. His words, not mine. He's been trying to set me up for the past couple of weeks and I am so over it." She pauses as the waiter brings her drink over. Taking a big gulp of it, her shoulders visibly sag in relief. "If I didn't love him so much I would've hurt him by now. Why can't people leave me alone, Marcello?"

I shrug and venture a guess. "Because they care?" I wince at the look she fires back. "Come on, Shark. Marcus loves you and sees how happy your sisters are. He just wants you to experience the same happiness. And Marcus being Marcus, he needs to be the one to give that to you. It's a shame he's gay or you two would be a perfect match."

She rolls her eyes and shakes her head. "Nope, we wouldn't work if he was straight. I'd kill him. I mean, IF I wanted a relationship, I'd want the real deal. The kind of love that people write about, you know? I'd want to be wrapped around each other, sickeningly enamoured with one another, and Marcus is far too exhausting for me to be around all of the time."

As I listen to her words, I watch her eyes cloud over with longing. I've learned that behind Shark's fierce facade is a heart as big as the ocean. She's ready to help everyone at the drop of a hat and will do whatever it takes to make her loved ones happy. But in all the time I've known her, she's never been in a relationship. Her sister reckons it's because she's a control freak, but I think there's something else.

"Would you want that, Em? A full on relationship?" I ask her hesitantly—this is Emilia Cooper after all, she'll think nothing of ripping my balls off.

She takes another sip of her drink and slowly places the glass down on the table. I'm just about to apologise for asking such a personal question when she responds.

"Maybe. I don't know. Sometimes I look at what my sisters have, Nell especially, and just think about what it'd be like if I had that too. Then I think back to all the pain she had to go through, the heartbreak…" She shakes her head and exhales a deep breath. "Nope. That's not for me. I don't need any more drama in my life. I have no time for it. Between you footballers, my sisters, and Marcus I have no energy left at all." She gives me an empty smile and I nod.

It seems I can hear what all the Cooper sisters are saying when they're silent, and not just Cleopatra. Before I can say anything else, Charlie and Zoe arrive and brother and sister-in-law time is over.

CHAPTER 31

Cleo

"I don't want a fucking spa day. Why are you making me do this?" I moan at my sisters in the back of Nell's car. I'm wedged in the middle seat as Juliet won rock paper scissors for the window seat and apparently Marcus gets car sick.

I scowl at my sister and then at Marcus too, who looks remarkably fine for someone who said he would practically die if he had to sit in the middle. I nudge them both with my elbows and put mine over theirs. Marcus nudges me back and fights to get his arm on top. Juliet leaves hers on the bottom, she knows not to push me today. Marcus, however, has been sent to test my patience. I nudge him harder this time and he chuckles and places his elbow on top of mine again. He uses his strength so I can't move mine and smirks smugly. A sweet smile flits across my face as I reach over, grab his nipple and twist it.

"Ow, no fair. You can't twist my nipples. Nell, Cleo's pinching me." Marcus squeals out as I comfortably rest my arm on top of his again.

"Cleo, Marcus, do not make me turn this car around and take you home," Nell shouts over her shoulder sharply.

"Oh please do, Nell. I didn't want to come, if you remember, so feel free to do just that," I reply.

Her shoulders sag and her head dips a little. "I know you didn't, Cleo. You've bitched enough about it for everyone to know. I just wanted to do something with just us as we haven't had sister time for a while now and I fucking miss you guys. I chose a spa because, unlike you lot, I don't get to pamper myself as often as I'd like. I have two small people who are very demanding and needy, and for once I wanted to do something just for me. But if you really want to go home, I'll take you. I don't want you to be miserable and moany all bloody day long."

Guilt washes over me and I hang my head in shame. "No, Nell. I'm sorry. You're right. Spending time with you guys is needed and you deserve to be pampered and spoiled. I'll stop moaning, I promise. But I get to sit by the window on the way home."

"Deal. Now stop pinching Marcus's nipples. And Marcus, let her arm be on top. You got the bloody window seat, stop winding her up."

Marcus whines at her scolding, mimicking her mockingly behind her back, but doesn't argue back. When he turns his aggrieved face to me, I present him with my saccharine sweetest smile. He sticks his tongue out and Juliet giggles, bringing out a chuckle from me as well.

Spending time with my sisters and Marcus is just what I need, even if it is in a bloody spa where I'll have to be social with people. At least I'll be all shiny and buffed for Antony tonight.

With that thought, I settle back into the middle seat and imagine all the naughty things he'll do to me—with my arms firmly resting on top of both of theirs.

CHAPTER 32

Can you feel the Cooper love? Group text

Will: Are you guys having fun?

Nell: We are. It's so nice to just be Nell for the day. I do miss you three though.

Connor: Aw we miss you too, Nell. Don't we Antony?

Antony: We do. We miss you so much.

Nell: Twats. I clearly meant Will and our children.

Connor: I'm hurt and shocked, Nell.

Antony: And you're supposed to be one of the nice Coopers.

Juliet: Am I the other nice one?

Connor: You're the best one (winking emoji, purple heart emoji)

Juliet: Awwww. I love you.

Emilia: Well that was rude, Connor.

Antony: Yes, you were Juliet.

Cleo: And what am I?

Antony: You want me to answer that on the family chat?

Cleo: Yep!

Antony: You're the Cooper sister that rocks my world. The one who was made just for me. The Cooper that's my opposite but who completes me. The missing piece of my puzzle

184

and the one who makes me want to do very dirty things to her. You're my sunflower.

Cleo:...

Nell: (Crying emoji, red love heart emoji, smiling emoji with love heart eyes)

Juliet: He made Nell speak emoji…

Emilia: Well damn, Marcello.

Will: Connor, we may need to up our game.

Connor: Fuck that. I got permanently marked for Juliet. Maybe you need to.

Will: Shit.

Will: Nell, I love you with so much of my heart that none is left to protest.

Nell: I love you too. How is Bea?

Will: And that is why I love you. You knew the quote, where it was from and the connection with Bea's name. She's fine, my lady.

Emilia: I knew the quote, where it was from and the connection to Bea's name too. Is that why you love me? (Laughing emoji)

Will: I love you for very different reasons, Em. Mainly for always having my back. Thank you. You're an amazing friend and sister.

Emilia: Well, okay then.

Nell: She's very articulate when she's emotional, isn't she?

Cleo: Do you see what you did, Antony? You made everyone lovey dovey and Emilia lose her articulation. My dad would be so mad (monkey covering its mouth emoji, red love heart emoji)

Marcus: What did I miss? I was having a massage.

Connor: Will and Antony were fighting it out for the 'most romantic' crown.

Marcus: You weren't competing?

Connor: Nah, I don't need that title.

Marcus: True. You're Mr. Growly, you don't need to be Mr. Most-Romantic as well lol.

Connor: FOM

Marcus: GRRRRRRRR

Antony: I'm going to need this story. It's the second time it's been brought up now…

Connor: No you don't.

Marcus: Changing the subject before Connor changes the locks on me…

Marcus: Which one of you had Mikel? I know one of you did.

Cleo: (Woman raising her hand emoji)

Marcus: Damn woman. He was a beautiful specimen of a man.

Cleo: He was.

Antony: WTF?

Nell: I'm disappointed, Antony. You couldn't type out 'What the fuck?'

Will: My lady, I think acronyms are the least of his worries right now.

Nell: Right!

Cleo: He was my massage therapist.

Antony: Cleopatra…

Cleo: He ran his big muscly hands all over me.

Antony: Stop!

Cleo: His fingers delved into every crevice and divot on my body.

Antony: This is a dangerous game to play, Sunflower. Especially on the chat we're on.

Cleo: I'm not playing any game. Just telling you who Mikel was and what he did to me…

Antony: Fine.

Will: Does that mean the same as it does when Nell says it?

Connor: Judging by his face, I'd say yes.

Cleo: Are you serious? Is he pissed off?

Cleo: Antony?

Cleo: Connor? Will?

Cleo: Antony!

Antony: I'm fine, Cleo. Hearing the woman you love talk about another man touching her is just fine.

Cleo: Shit! You used Cleo. I'm sorry. I was just playing. I didn't even get a massage.

Cleo: Please don't be mad at me.

Cleo: I'm sorry.

Antony: Okay, Sunflower.

Cleo: Just like that?

Antony: Yep. I told you it was a dangerous game to play on here…

Cleo: Fucker!

Juliet: I never thought I'd see the day Cleo was all in a tizzie over a man.

Cleo: I wasn't in a tizzie, Princess.

Nell: Yeah you were.

Emilia: Complete tizzie.

Marcus: Tizzie temptress

Cleo: FUCK OFF, ALL OF YOU!

Antony: Dangerous game, Sunflower. See you later Cleopatra (Love heart emoji)

CHAPTER 33

Work is busy. I'm swimming in events. The newspapers wrote about 'our quaint little events company' planning Zoe and Charlie's party, and since then we've been inundated with requests for meetings. People are scrambling to get in our books. It's created quite a bit of chaos around here.

Princess is doing really well, and has been a huge help. With her flair for organising, she's able to manage the smaller events and corporate lunches on her own, leaving the larger affairs to me. I was a little worried at first, but honestly, I felt like a proud parent the first time she did an event without me. Especially when the next time they booked in, they asked for her specifically. She squealed like a pig for about ten seconds solid. It was annoying but adorable at the same time.

And even though my bank account is grateful for all of the revenue these extra events are bringing in, I miss Verity. She's my partner in all of this and should be here reaping the benefits with me. This was our dream. She still has no idea when she'll be back, as she's having far too much fun with JP, but she's ecstatic about how well business is going.

"Sunflower, you ready for lunch? There's paparazzi outside,

so keep your hands off me or they'll know that the most eligible bachelor in football is taken." Antony winks at me and stands in my office, looking sexy as fuck in a black shirt, open at the collar, with his sunflower pin attached. He's worn that thing every day since the first time he got it and I love him for it.

I don't love that the paparazzi have been camped outside for days now. I also don't love the idea of hiding our relationship again, but I'm not ready to have my face splashed all over the tabloids.

"I am. There's been paparazzi outside ever since that stupid newspaper reported about my 'quaint little company.' Wankers. I know they were being sarcastic arseholes about us because we aren't an established company." He's heard my venting since the article was published, but he still always listens.

"I know, Sunflower. The press are twats when they want to be. They can be good though. There's a black tie event that I've been invited to and the publicity the press will generate will double the exposure for the charities involved. Will you come with me?"

I nod then stop and do a double take. "What? Come where?"

"To the event? I want to make us red carpet official. I want everyone to know you're my sunflower and I'm your twatface." He reaches out, takes my hand, and nausea swirls in the pit of my stomach.

The whole world watches those events. The celebrities and sports stars who attend are splashed all over every newspaper and magazine. Reporters and critics debate over who's dressed the best and who's dating who. I've read those articles. Am I ready to *be* an article? I've seen the spin they put on things. They'll probably make out I only got Charlie and Zoe's party because I'm sleeping with Antony. They'll post my picture next to his and everyone will question what he's doing with me.

What if he reads them and starts to think the same? No, he wouldn't. He's got rose tinted glasses on when it comes to us. Take the past few days—I've barely had time to see him, and when I have, I've been sullen and tired. Not ideal girlfriend material. But he hasn't moaned once. He hasn't told me to shut up or to be happier. He's just let me vent and get whatever's bugging me off my chest. I've been snarky, snappy, and snide to him. The Queen of Darkness has been out in full force and he hasn't batted an eyelid. He's stayed his chirpy, sunshiny self. The man deserves a medal for putting up with me.

"Antony, I'm not ready for that yet." I watch his smile slip and his eyes dim. He quickly schools his face back into happy Antony mode, but I saw the glitch in his facade. I did that to him. Again. It was the same look he gave me in the car park on Connor's birthday. The one that tells me I was right and I'm not cut out for this relationship crap.

"Okay, Cleopatra. We'll wait. It's okay. You ready to go?" He doesn't reach for me, or try to take my hand, just simply hangs back and waits for me to grab my coat.

I turn to him as I sweep my hair out of my collar and say, "Maybe after the engagement party we can go official with the press. That way they can't put a nasty spin on us."

He smiles tightly. "It's fine, Cleo. You're worried about the press, I get it. Let's go." He spins away from me and my heart cracks. He called me Cleo. Fuck.

CHAPTER 34

Antony

"Antony, Antony! Look this way. Where's your date? How's the ankle? Antony! Antony." Flashing lights are blinding me but I smile continuously and pose like I've been trained to, silently wishing the red carpet would open up and swallow me whole.

The last place I want to be is standing here with the UK press hounds asking me question after question about my ankle, football and lovelife. I would much prefer being at home, snuggled up to Cleopatra on our sofa, but she's been avoiding me since our lunch date a few days ago. All of a sudden she's too busy to talk, too busy to see me, too busy for me in general.

I know I got a little frustrated with her and that's why she's retreating again. *She* backs off when she thinks *I'm* going to, a defence mechanism to help her cope for when I 'leave.' What she fails to realise is that I'm not going anywhere, I'm not leaving.

It's making me even more determined to propose to her and show her we have the forever kind of love and not the fleeting kind. That I'm not calling time on us, no matter how snarky she is and how much she retreats. It's all planned. I've spoken to her mum and dad—not to ask permission, because we all know Cleo is her own person and she's the only one who can say yes to marrying me, more to just let them know what my intentions are. I've finally got all of the Coopers involved. I had to leave telling Juliet and Connor till the last minute because Juliet is the worst secret keeper and Connor can't keep anything from her. They're all on board and excited to be a part of it. Even Charlie has come around to the idea and helped me make a playlist for the big moment. I'm going to decorate Nell's front room in tacky red heart balloons, a throwback to one of our earlier conversations about how to decorate romantically. I think she'll get a kick out of it.

This Saturday, in front of all her family, I'll ask the most important question of my life. I just hope I get the answer I want.

"Antony?" I turn my head to see Trudy Sellers, a friend of Zoe's from her reality show, approach me. I spot her girl-friend, Sadie, waiting in the wings for her. As she embraces me in a hug and air kisses each of my cheeks I offer a sad smile at Sadie. Not everyone knows Trudy's gay, she's scared to come out, and I suddenly feel an affinity with Sadie. She smiles back but it doesn't reach her eyes as Trudy grabs my arm and places it around her waist. She whispers without moving her lips, "Take a few pictures with me. It'll stop them asking who she is and why I came with a 'friend'."

I smile broadly and place my arm around her shoulders instead of her waist—it's a less intimate embrace—and pose with her for a few seconds. She laughs and plays up for the cameras, grinning mischievously when the reporters ask if we're dating. She's leaning into me as I stand rigid next to her. I don't want to make a scene and bring further attention to myself, which would ultimately bring it to Cleopatra as well. When I shrug her arm off my shoulder, she just laughs and tiptoes to try to place a kiss on my cheek. I turn my head away and flinch as her lips brush my ear. The reporters and photographers are catching all of this.

Sadie approaches as I walk away from the red carpet. I can see the pain in her eyes and an apologetic smile on her lips. She envelops me in a bear hug. "Antony, how are you?"

I squeeze back, tightly, wanting her to know I see her. "I'm good. I'm dating an incredible woman."

"So am I." Trudy places her hand on Sadie's shoulder and, although she's smiling, the slight flinch when Trudy touches her is apparent. I smile politely at them both and excuse myself. I have enough complications of my own, I'm not getting involved in anyone else's.

I walk to a quiet corner and bring up Cleopatra's information. I know this is a televised live auction and I don't want her to get the wrong end of the stick seeing me with Trudy. My call goes to voicemail but I still smile when I hear Cleopatra's voice telling me "You know what to do…" and the beep that follows.

"Sunflower, I just wanted to call and remind you that I love you. I don't know if you're watching this or not, but if you see me with Trudy, please don't think anything of it. She's a friend of Zoe's and we've met a few times before. She's always chasing a headline. I wish you were here with me. Whatever you're doing, have a lovely night and I'll see you later hopefully? Let me know. Love you, *Girasole*."

I hang up, feeling marginally better. I know she has insecurities, and who can blame her after what that fucktwat did to her. So, if I have to reassure her on a night like tonight, I will.

I straighten my sunflower pin on my lapel and take a deep breath as I head inside and find my place at the table. I hate these events, but they're good for my image and it helps the charities gain extra revenue when athletes and celebrities attend. I smile at Charlie and Zoe who are sitting opposite me and notice the seat next to me has been left empty. Good, I don't want anyone sitting there except Cleopatra.

I sip at my water and anxiously check my phone. Still no message from her. I hope that doesn't mean what I think it does. I type out a text to her, trying to convey just how much I miss her right now.

Antony: I hope you got my voicemail. If not, listen to it please. I love you, Sunflower X

Antony: I forgot to tell you, I miss you. Can I see you later, Cleopatra? X

I leave my phone on the table next to my water and pray that it lights up with a response from my *girasole*, my sunflower.

CHAPTER 35

Cleo

We're gathered in Nell's front room, watching the charity auction that Antony is at, waiting to get a glimpse of him. We've already seen Charlie and Zoe arrive on the red carpet and they both looked stunning. Zoe's long, pale, pink dress fit her like a second skin. Complemented by the pale pink tie that Charlie wore with his white tuxedo jacket with black lapels, they look like the ultimate power couple. Marcus and Juliet shrieked at the same time, "We know them!" making everyone laugh. All except me.

I feel guilty for not being there. I just couldn't bring myself to be exposed like that, and after he called me Cleo the other day, I know he's slipping away from me. It's why I've kept myself busy these past couple of days. I'm trying to keep him at a distance so I can manage the heartache and humiliation better. I frown at the pillow I'm cuddling to my chest and jump when Princess squeals like a pig and shakes my arm.

"It's him. Cleo, look."

I force my eyes to the screen and manage to get out of her grip. When I see him, my heart constricts in my chest. He's beautiful. His brown eyes twinkle with each flash of light from the cameras, but there's no fire behind them. His smile gets wider with every head tilt he gives them. Questions about his ankle and football infiltrate my hazy brain and I listen half heartedly to his answers. My attention is caught on him. The sadness in his eyes that flashes through when a reporter asks why he's alone almost breaks me. I choke back a sob when he reaches up to his lapel and subconsciously fiddles with his sunflower pin. I'm reaching for my phone, wanting to hear his voice, when a blonde bitch sidles up next to him and he drops his hand from his pin to embrace her.

"WHAT THE ACTUAL FUCK?" I fume out and forget that the whole room is filled with my family. Emilia chuckles and my head whips around so quickly I think I've done myself an injury. "What's so fucking funny?" I ask through gritted teeth.

She throws her head back and cackles at me and the only thing stopping me from launching myself at her is Juliet's grip on my arm.

"Calm the fuck down, Little Miss Jealous. Green isn't a good shade on you," Emilia retorts nonchalantly, and when I growl at her she just chuckles more.

"Emilia, stop it," Nells firm voice scolds.

Emilia sighs. "Fine. What I say can go no further though, Coopers. Agree?" Murmurs of yes and of course flitter through the room and I stare at Emilia, willing her to speak faster.

"That woman is Trudy Sellers." Before I can tell her I know her fucking name, she continues. "She's gay. It's not known outside of the industry, but she's obviously seen an opportunity with Antony to throw people off track and make them question whether they're together or not." She looks pointedly at me. "He looked just as shocked as you were to see her. If you hadn't been shooting eye daggers at me, you would have seen him remove his arm from her waist and put it around her shoulders. He turned his head and visibly shuddered when she tried to kiss his cheek. You have no reason to feel jealous. Stupid and guilty maybe, but not jealous." She cuts me a dirty look, leans forward, and takes a sip of her drink.

My brow furrows at her in anger and hurt. I throw the pillow down and place my hands on my hips. "What does that mean?" I ask, fury seeping through every pore of my being.

"You shouldn't doubt him, Cleo. He wouldn't do that to you. And you should've been with him. If you had, she wouldn't have been able to capitalise on him being alone." She smugly sits back, smiling as I slump into my chair and stick my tongue out at her, all the fight I had in me gone.

"I didn't want to go. I don't want to be in the limelight," I stroppily bite out at them.

"Wait a minute," Marcus pipes up, and I roll my eyes knowing that what comes next is going to annoy me. "You were invited and didn't want to go? You're dating a professional footballer and don't want to be in the limelight? Honey, that's not possible," he says and the rest of them join in.

"I mean, Cooper, come on. You must've known when you started dating him the press would find out," Connor adds.

"It's okay to be nervous about being in the public eye, Cleo. I would be too. But what you and Antony have is special and can withstand that. Just give them your Queen of Darkness look and you'll be fine. The press will back off immediately." Juliet tries to reassure me, and I love her for it, but I don't want the whole world knowing I'm dating him. Not yet.

I smile at her but don't respond. I let them each talk amongst themselves. All of them except Emilia make a comment about not being able to date a celebrity and remain private. I know they're right but I wish they knew why I had these reservations. That I'm terrified of screwing this relationship up and the whole world knowing about it and being humiliated all over again but on a wider scale this time. I look up and catch Emilia's gaze. She mouths "Sorry" and I mouth back "Me too."

My phone starts to ring and distracts me from my thoughts. Antony's name flashes across my screen. I silence the call and let it go to voicemail. I can't talk to him when I'm all muddled up. I need to get my emotions in check. Emilia's right. I shouldn't have questioned him and I should've been with him, but imagine if I had told the world I was his and she'd approached him like that. The headlines the next day would have been 'Antony Marcello dating blonde bombshell' and I would've looked like an absolute idiot. I can't deal with that again. A notification pops up telling me I have a voice message to listen to and I silently sneak away to hear it.

I lock the bathroom door and let the tears slide down my face as I listen to him call me sunflower in Italian. I desperately want this anxiety and fear to go away so I can enjoy this time with him but I don't know how to make it disappear. A text from him comes through and a sad smile takes over my lips. He deserves so much more than what I can offer him. I type back a reply.

Cleo: I'm fine. You looked hot! Everything's fine. I'm staying at Nell's tonight so I'll see you tomorrow? X

Footsteps on the landing notify me that my sisters are outside. I hear the shuffling and whispering about who should knock on the door. Wiping the tears away, I fix a smile on my face and open the door before they figure out who gets the honour.

"What's up?" I ask them, not a trace of emotion in my voice.

"We thought you were upset." Juliet tells me, and I broaden my smile to prove her wrong.

"Nope, I just wanted to listen to Antony's message and send one back. Didn't want you all to hear what I intend to do with him when I next see him, that's all." As I move past them, I catch Emilia's eye and she subtly reaches out her hand and brushes her fingers along mine. The Cooper Circle of Comfort needs to be completed by her.

"Come on, let's see how much money Antony spends. Marcus better not have eaten all the fucking popcorn." I walk downstairs with my game face on. I can't let them see the pain inside, so I smile and act like everything is fine, whilst a river of turmoil rages through me.

CHAPTER 36
Antony

I wait for the call to connect but again it goes straight through to voicemail. I've tried calling her a thousand times and, apart from the text telling me she was 'fine', she hasn't responded to me. I know she saw Trudy's little show but I was hoping she knew me well enough to know I wouldn't do anything like that to her. She does. I know she does. She's just got to let go of her demons.

I hate that she's staying at Nell's tonight and I can't see her. If she'd been at home I would've gone straight over, but I can't risk waking Bea and Ben up. What kind of an uncle would I be then?

My phone rings and I quickly glance down at it and sigh loudly when I see Papa's name flash on the screen.

"Ciao, Papa. You okay?" I ask. Before I can finish my sentence I hear him raging at me in Italian. "Papa, slow down. I can't understand what you're saying. Calm down."

I speak fluent Italian, I spent most of my childhood between London and Stresa, lake Magorrie in the North of Italy where Papa is from, but when he gets in a rant, he may as well be speaking an alien language as I can't understand a thing. I manage to catch a few words - *blonda, tradire, idiota* and *deluso*. His words fuel a rage within me that's stoked by hurt. He saw the auction tonight and thinks I was cheating on Cleopatra. He should know his son better than that.

"You really think that highly of me, don't you? You think I'd *cheat* on Cleopatra, live on TV with some *blonde*? That I'm a *delusional idiot*? I'm hurt, Papa." I let the pain filter through my voice and hear him sigh.

"I'm sorry, *Mio figlio*. I shouldn't have lost my temper. I should've listened first. I got angry, I thought you were jeopardising your own future. Your mama wasn't here to talk sense to me. Be my voice of reason."

Even though I'm irritated with him, I blow out a resigned breath and reassure him, "It's fine, Papa. I know it's because you care. That lady was a friend of Zoe's who saw her chance to get some headlines. It's not uncommon. It's one of the pitfalls of being a footballer. Unfortunately, you can't just play the game on the field, you have to be famous and play that game too."

I grab the back of my neck as Charlie and Zoe walk toward me. Charlie mouths, "You ready to go?" and I nod but put my finger up, indicating one minute.

"Papa, I have to go. I'm leaving the event now and the press are outside. I don't want to be on the phone when I leave."

"Okay, but first tell me. Did your Cleopatra see that and was she okay? Your mama would've been ready to kill me if that had been me when we were younger. Hell, still would today." He chuckles and I grin knowing full well that my mama is ridiculously jealous, even after all these years.

"I don't know, Papa. I left her a message straight after and told her about it, so I'm hoping she's okay. Especially after what I have planned for her Saturday."

I can hear his smile through the phone as he speaks. "Make sure you go to her tomorrow. Make her know what she saw isn't the truth. You'll phone us as soon as she says yes. And you'll fly over as soon as you both can?"

"Yes, Papa. We will. I have to go. Charlie's waiting for me. He says hi."

"You tell him I said hi back, but tell Zoe I said she looked beautiful tonight." I laugh at his flattery and tell them both. Charlie frowns as Zoe giggles at Papa's compliment and I roll my eyes at all of them.

I hang up and affix a smile to my face as we leave as a trio and the flashes assault my eyes again. My hands are in my pockets, clutching hold of the phone so I'll feel the vibrations if she rings, but she doesn't. And the determination for Saturday to go ahead ramps up a level in my head. She will be mine.

CHAPTER 37

Cleo

It's Friday, the day after the bloody auction. I've checked the newspaper headlines obsessively and Antony only features slightly. Trudy, however, does not. She's the main headline in every newspaper.

From what I can gather, there was an altercation between her and her girlfriend. Seems she was caught discussing the idea of faking a romance with a male celebrity to further her career. Apparently she wants to be taken more seriously and get into acting. Someone filmed her and Sadie arguing about it and sold it to the press.

It's horrible and I feel so bad for Sadie. They've delved into every aspect of their relationship, even going as far as speaking to her old teachers and so-called friends. It's a vile intrusion of their privacy, but I can't stop reading about them. It's like a car crash that you want to look away from but can't.

I keep focusing on the comments underneath the articles. Comment after comment with vile hurtful words about them being gay and Trudy being able to do better. How they're glad they've broken up and that Sadie wasn't good enough. How must she feel this morning? She's nursing a broken heart and facing public humiliation to boot. I slam the mouse of my computer down hard and push away from my desk.

"Woah, what's the matter, Cleo?" Juliet's voice floats through my anger and I shake my head. I tell her what I've been reading.

"They're just gutter trash papers. The people commenting are vile homophobic imbeciles and aren't worth wasting your energy on."

Whilst I agree with her, I still can't shake my irritation.

My phone rings from my desk drawer but I ignore it. I know it's Antony. I want to speak to him but I also have a lot of work to get on with. That's my story and I'm sticking with it.

Except, in reality, I feel guilty that I judged him and scared that I'm just not enough, that I can't give him enough.

As the call rings off, Juliet raises an eyebrow and I shrug my shoulders. I focus my sights and energy on her work-space. "You need to tidy your bloody desk. It's a mess." Distraction used to work on her when she was a kid but she's gotten older and smarter, unfortunately.

She blows out a breath, the frustration clear as anything in her groan. "I need more on my desk than a screen, keyboard and mouse. Nice try at the distraction tactic, but what is going on with you, Cleo?"

I'm about to answer when a voice sucks all the air from the room. And my lungs.

"I was wondering the same thing, Juliet. Tell me, Sunflower, is it just me you're ignoring on the phone today or is it everyone?" Antony stands in the office doorway, his arms crossed over his chest, glaring at me. I gulp at the fierceness of his expression and get aroused at the same time. It's the same look he gets when he's dominating me in the bedroom. It's fucking hot, but right now I have some explaining to do.

"Juliet, could you give us a minute?"

"Yep, absolutely. I'll work from home today. Take as long as you need." She grabs her things quickly, making a bee-line for the door. As she steps behind him she mouths, "Sort it out."

I lower my lashes to let her know I see. She has her phone in her hands before she's even out the door and I know she's going to text everyone. I roll my eyes at the thought of the teasing and explaining I'll have to do.

"I don't think now is the time for rolling those beautiful eyes of yours, *Girasole*."

Hearing him speak Italian makes my heart flutter. I want to strip naked for him, right here in my office, but I don't. Instead I nervously tell him, "I wasn't rolling them at you. I saw Juliet texting everyone about this..." I try to explain myself but I trail off as he turns around, locks the main office door, and turns back to me, silently.

I can't take my eyes off him as he stalks over to me. He's barely limping anymore but the thud of his boot is loud in the silent space. I step back slightly and the backs of my knees hit my desk. He closes the hallway door and locks that too. There's just me and him now. He strides toward me, stopping right in front of me, silence filling the empty space around us.

"Antony. What are you doing?" I whisper.

"Why were you ignoring me, Cleopatra?" He strokes his hand up and down my arm. Feather light touches flit over the bare skin exposed by my short sleeved shirt and shivers race through my body.

"I felt guilty. For not being there with you. So I shut down. I'm still trying to understand how to process my emotions. I'm sorry." My voice has taken on this ethereal whisper. His touches are causing a frenzy of need within me.

He steps closer, his body pressing against mine, and I purr when I feel his erection digging into me.

"Shhh. I know. I told you I'm listening, even when you're silent. I missed you last night though. Not just at the event. I missed having you in my bed." He brings his lips to my collarbone and licks a trail up my throat. I shiver when his breath tickles the shell of my ear and moan when he nips it with his teeth.

"I missed the taste of your sweet honey coating my tongue. I missed your tight, pink nipples urging me to take them in my mouth. I missed your lips. Your tongue. You. I don't like it when you ignore me, Cleopatra. Don't do it again. Please?" This whole time he's been talking with his lips brushing my ear and his body pressed against me. I'm so turned on I feel like I could come at any second.

"I won't. I promise. I missed you too,," I breathe out and wrap my arms around his neck. He groans as my skin touches his. He lifts me onto my desk and one by one he meticulously undoes the buttons of my shirt. He trails his lips across the tops of my breasts. I groan and arch my back, seeking the heat of his mouth on my nipple. He skips over them and places feather light kisses on my stomach. As he rolls my skirt up my thighs, I lift up so he can push it up further. A smile creeps onto my face as I hear his sudden intake of breath. He just discovered I'm not wearing anything underneath the skirt.

"This is very naughty, Sunflower. First you ignore me and now I learn you've been here all morning with your pussy bare. Very, very naughty." He smirks and dips his head.

I lay back on my desk. "You'll have to punish me then, won't you?"

He smiles against the inside of my thigh and glides his tongue along the sensitive skin until I can feel his breath on my mound. He inhales and moans. Gripping my thighs tightly, he lowers himself onto a chair then pulls me so my bum is hanging off the desk and flips my legs over his shoulders. The first long slow lick of his tongue has me crying out in ecstasy. I bury my fingers into his hair as he laps my juices up slowly and deliberately. As he focuses on my clit with little flicks of his tongue, I start to feel the first burst of my orgasm. Just as I'm about to tip over the edge, he stops.

I grip his hair tightly and pull myself up on my elbows so I can look down at him.

"What the fuck?"

He smirks and asks, "Are you going to ignore me again, Sunflower?"

I huff out a frustrated, "No."

"Good, I don't like being ignored. And I definitely don't like not having you come on my tongue."

I'm about to argue that I don't either but his mouth is back lapping at my pussy, and this time there is nothing slow about it. He's devouring me. As his teeth nip at my clit, his fingers plunge inside of me. I groan out his name as he thrusts his fingers in the same rhythm as his tongue fucks me. I'm flying higher and higher. With one final suck of my clit, I see fireworks.

CHAPTER 38

Antony

I wipe the hair off her forehead and place my lips on hers. I love this woman so fucking much. I don't care if she struggles with her emotions. The more I keep showing up for her when she tries to push me away, the more she will understand that I'm going nowhere and she's it for me.

She opens her eyes and smiles up at me. "Thank you. I'm sorry."

I shake my head at her and kiss her forehead. "You don't need to be sorry. I understand why you didn't want to attend the auction. I'm sorry I got frustrated with you before our lunch the other day. I know why you don't want to be in the public eye. Believe me, Cleopatra, I don't either. Unfortunately my job requires it though." With another quick kiss to her lips I help her to sit up.

I start to button her shirt and she asks me, "We aren't finished are we?"

Even though it's agony for me to cover her perfect breasts up, I don't want to monopolise her whole working day. I could easily lay her back down and spend the whole day worshipping her, but I know how much she has to do.

"For now, yes, Sunflower. You have work to get on with. I hope after that you won't be as stressed about it." I grin.

She smirks back and purrs, "I am definitely less stressed, Antony. And later on, I'm going to rock your world, Baby."

A chuckle escapes from my lips. I stop myself from telling her that she always does and wink at her instead.

Once I know she's dressed, I unlock the doors and sit on the other side of her desk as she brings her computer back to life. She grunts about someone being a twat and I tilt my head at her. I'm intrigued to know who or what has annoyed her so much in the space of seconds.

"Sorry, I was reading some of the papers, to see if you were in them, and the story they ran on Trudy and Sadie is just awful."

I shake my head at her, letting her know I have no clue what she's talking about, so she spins the screen around for me to see.

Once I've read the article and the comments beneath it, I turn it back. I know she was studying my face for a reaction. Her eyes were boring into me whilst I was reading, and although I agree with her and think it's a disgusting article, I don't let my features reveal that little bit of information. I keep my face neutral and shrug. I don't want to fuel her hatred of the press, I need her to get over it if I want her to be my wife. And I really do want her to be my wife.

"Unfortunately that's one of the pitfalls of being 'famous.' You have to remember though, Sunflower, this is what Trudy has worked her whole career for. She'll be in her element with all of this exposure." I'm not lying when I say that. Trudy's the kind of person who would do anything to stay relevant and in the public eye. She craves fame and fortune and won't stop until she's got it.

"But what about Sadie? She didn't ask for all of this. She just fell in love with someone who just happened to be famous. She shouldn't be dragged through the mud like this."

She's sitting forward, readying herself for battle. I study her, listening to her words and listening when she's silent. Whilst I don't doubt she's upset for Sadie, I also know there's an element of fear too. I have to be very careful with my words now and make sure she knows the differences between the two of them.

"I agree, she doesn't, but Trudy handled their relationship all wrong. She hid Sadie away like she was ashamed of her. She lied about her sexuality for years and wanted to lie to the press and her fans about a sham relationship." As much as the press is to blame, so is Trudy. She threw Sadie under the bus the minute she denied their relationship.

"Why does she have to come out though? Why do people care who she's dating? That's the real issue here. The press think they're owed something because you're famous." She's getting more and more angry as the conversation continues.

"Because that's what you sign up for when you sell your soul for fame. I know it's hard to understand, but that's the way it is. I don't crave the spotlight like Trudy does but I still have it on me. And I knew if I made it professionally and achieved my dreams I'd have to make a choice about my 'celebrity' status. Would I be a Trudy, craving it and seeking publicity everywhere I went, or would I be an Antony?"

I grin at her and I'm rewarded with a roll of her eyes so I continue. "I never wanted to be famous, but I did want to be a footballer. The press don't hound me and Charlie half as much as they do Brady because we don't seek out the atten-tion. If I were in Trudy's situation, I would've been honest with everyone. I would've picked a reporter I knew, trusted to an extent, and given them the story of my relationship. Let them know I was dating an amazing woman that I adored. I wouldn't care what anyone else thought about it either. From my experience with the press, the more you hide from them, the more they dig. If it's worth hiding, it's worth a story."

My eyes don't leave hers with every word that comes out of my mouth. I watch as her face screws up in concentration, trying to decide whether she agrees or not. I watch as she bristles at the mention of telling everyone about my relationship. And I watch as the admiration flashes through her eyes when I say I wouldn't care about others' opinions.

"You make some excellent points, Twatface."

I tip my head to her in acceptance of her compliment. She wants us just as much as I do. She wants the forever kind. And it's my job to help her get through the fear of humiliation and loss and make her see that I'm hers. Forever.

CHAPTER 39

The unproposal - group text

Antony: Is everything ready?

Marcus: Yes. But I don't know why you left this to me, Connor, and Will to do.

Antony: I can't keep going to her sisters about everything. She didn't like it when I told Shark stuff about her.

Connor: Why?

Emilia: Why?

Marcus: Why?

Marcus: Jinx

Antony: @Shark it gave you the edge over her and you told Nell everything and she told your mum. Apparently Cleopatra spent ten minutes on the phone talking about our great love affair - before we were even dating!

Connor: Oh Nell, that was sly. I fucking love it!

Nell: She was annoying me. We all knew she had a thing for Twatface, no offence.

Antony: None taken.

Nell: I was trying to force her hand.

Emilia: As was I. Hence why I told you in the first place. We all know I'm the best secret keeper in this family.

Antony: Hence why I took you ring shopping.

Will: Nell and Juliet moaned about that when they found out.

Antony: I didn't mean any offence, ladies.

Nell: We didn't moan, we were slightly vexed.

Juliet: No, Nell. We moaned. Loudly. About the injustice of not being invited.

Nell: Fine!

Emilia: I can't help being the chosen one, ladies.

Marcus: You should have taken me. She wouldn't have been annoyed by that.

Antony: Hopefully she won't be annoyed at all. She'll be so happy to be engaged…

Connor: You keep thinking that lol

Juliet: Connie, don't be mean.

Will: Anyway. Everything is set up. The kids are with the grandparents and the girls will be here soon. Won't you?

Antony: Thanks guys. I really appreciate all of this. I wish I was there to help but I couldn't miss my scan.

Nell: Yes, we'll be there in about an hour. Is that okay, Antony?

Antony: Perfect. I'm almost there so we'll be waiting for you to all enter.

Marcus: Aren't you scared she'll say no?

Antony: Nah, if she says no, I'll keep asking her until she says yes.

Connor: Best answer ever.

Will: Things done well and with a care, exempt themselves from fear…

Marcus: What?

Connor: I think it's a Shakespeare quote.

Nell: It is! Mr. Shakespeare strikes again.

Antony: I kinda get that one.

Marcus: I don't.

Will: It's saying if you care enough about what you're doing, you'll take care doing it and there won't be a need for fear.

Marcus: You're so ducking clever.

Will: Nah, I didn't write it. Shakespeare's the clever one.

Nell: He is ducking clever, Marcus.

Connor: Okay, so we're all in agreement that Will is ducking clever. Can we move on. Let's get my bestie engaged.

Antony: (fingers crossed emoji)

CHAPTER 40
Cleo

Is everyone acting weird or am I just in a funky mood? I guess either, or both, could be true.

I was hoping Antony and his little impromptu visit and the mind blowing orgasm he gave me would help me get over my doubts and fears about being shoved into the limelight, but no such luck.

After I'd come down from my orgasmic bliss and settled down to work, all I could think about was Sadie. How she fell in love and got screwed over by everyone, including the person she loved.

It reminded me of Alex, what he did to me, and how the whole campus looked at me with pity.

I keep imagining that happening on a world wide scale. Everyone having an opinion on you and your relationship, strangers judging you and feeling sorry for you. Thankfully, I only had to deal with the humiliation side of things before, no heartbreak. But this time I'd be devastated at losing Antony. My heart wouldn't just be broken, more like shattered into a thousand pieces. Throw into the mix public annihilation via the press and every Tom, Dick and Harry, and I don't think I'd be able to cope. The idea of the whole world judging me, seeing pictures of me hiding behind sunglasses, too ashamed to show my red, swollen, tearfilled eyes. It's all too much. Clients, family, friends, exes all judging me and my life choices. No. I can't do it. I can't be in a public relationship with Antony. No matter how much I want him, I can't put myself on the line like that.

"Is it time to go yet?" Juliet asks and receives a kick under the table for it.

"Ow, that really hurt, Nell," she grunts as she rubs her shin. Nell looks at her through narrowed eyes. Juliet sits up straighter than a soldier on parade and starts to fiddle with her hair and now I know something's up.

"What the fuck is going on? Nell, why did you kick her under the table and why are you playing with your hair? Spill. Now." I point my finger and zone my attention onto Princess because I know she's the weakest link when it comes to divulging information. She shifts in her seat under my scrutiny, her eyes flitting between each of me and our sisters. I glare at her.

She whimpers and I hear Emilia's sigh from next to me. "You're going to make her cry, for God's sake. I'll tell you what's going on but leave Princess alone."

I watch as both Nell's and Juliet's eyes widen and their jaws drop in shock. Emilia's the best secret keeper in the family. Why is she suddenly divulging information willingly? I relent my scowl from Juliet's eyes and raise an eyebrow at Emilia.

"Antony is meeting us back at Nell's. He wasn't sure if he'd make it in time after his scan but he finished early. He wanted to surprise you as he's boot free. Just make a big deal about it to him, please, so he doesn't know I've ruined the surprise. I don't want him pouting about it. I have enough of that with Marcus."

"That's it?" Emilia nods as Nell and Juliet stand up and

ask if we're ready to leave again. "Yeah, okay. But you guys are definitely acting weird."

I hear Emilia chuckle behind me as we exit the restaurant where we've just finished dinner. "You're the one who was in her head the whole way through our meal. I don't think it's just us that are acting weird, Sis."

I don't reply. She's absolutely right and I don't want to have to explain what was going through my mind. I know they won't understand and I don't want to be the fucked up sister, not after the lectures I gave Juliet and Nell for being so secretive about their own issues.

Instead, I shrug my shoulders and put a smile on my face, looping arms with Juliet. She smiles and I place a kiss on her cheek, my way of apologising for making her squirm earlier. Great, now she's grinning and I roll my eyes because I know they're all acting weirdly. But any further questions from me will cause further questions from them. And I want to avoid that at all costs.

The drive back to Nell's is an uneventful trip. We talk about Verity, Ben and Bea, and Emilia even opens up about her boss's imminent retirement and how the idea puts her on edge. It's nice to just be with my sisters for a change. It's been a long time since we've done anything like this.

As we pull up to Nell's, I'm oblivious to the delay tactics my sisters have put in place as we exit the car. I don't realise how slowly they're walking behind me so I reach the front door before them. I don't immediately register the gasps of breath as I fling the door open to see a million red hearts strung all over Nell's hallway. I don't flinch when I feel three hands gently pressing my lower back to make my feet move. I don't recognize the noises behind me as I'm manoeuvred into the living room where more red hearts are displayed all throughout the room. I can't acknowledge the thud of my heart racing in my chest at the sight of Antony kneeling in front of me.

I won't look at what he's holding in his hand. Instead I look at his beautiful face. His eyes shining with love and a smile that's as wide as the ocean. I hear the words, "Will you marry me?" and everything comes crashing around me. The red balloons that we joked about, the fear, the shame, the humiliation, the doubts, the fleeting kind of girl I've always been.

"I-I can't. I'm sorry."

I run.

I turn on my heel and leave this beautiful, amazing, unicorn of a man on his knee in the middle of the floor.

I run through the kitchen and into the back garden and the floodgates that normally keep my emotions at bay fly open. I can't control them and I don't want to. I've held them all in check for too long. I slink to the ground, bringing my knees up tightly to my chest. I've just ruined everything. He'll never want me again. I broke his heart and for what?

I'm completely unaware I've uttered that question aloud until I hear Nell say, "That's what we want to know too, Cleo."

I bring my head up to see my three sisters standing there. I try to get words to come out of my mouth, but before I can, the door opens and we're joined by Marcus, Connor and Will.

"Guys, I think this is a sister thing."

"No." Connor shuts Emilia down firmly. "We've been pushed to the sidelines for this Cooper Circle of Comfort for too long now. We're all Coopers here. We're all a part of the circle. We all want to comfort her. Deal?"

I watch in awe as my sisters nod their heads and Connor scoops me up and places me on one of the garden chairs. Nell sits next to me on one side, Emilia on the other and Juliet stands behind me with a hand on each shoulder. Marcus stands next to Emilia's chair and Will next to Nell. But it's Connor who squats in front of me, his hand on my knee, and his blue eyes searing into mine. Concern and worry crash in them and I can't take it. All of them want to be here for me and instead of feeling embarrassed or ashamed, I'm comforted by just how much these people love me. They aren't judging me, just trying to understand what is going on in my head.

"What *is* going on, Cleo?" Connor asks gently.

This time I can't keep it all in anymore. I lower my eyes to my lap and spill my guts to my family. I tell them everything about Alex the fucktwat, about not being made for the forever kind and about the fear of humiliation. About not wanting them to know I fucked up and being embarrassed by feeling like that.

"Why didn't you tell us? I knew something happened in uni. I would've done something had I known, Cooper." Connor's words wash over me as I look up at him and smile.

"I know you would've Coop-hay. I didn't want you to know. You had enough going on in your life. Plus it happened a little bit before we lost Steve and everything was rubbish for everyone."

Juliet tightens her grip on my shoulder and I reach up to squeeze her hand reassuringly. "Cleo, we're your family. We love you and always will. You've been there for each of us and we would never judge you. EVER!" I look up to see Juliet's eyes fill with tears as she speaks, and instead of feeling like she's pitying me, I know she's empathising with me.

"Coopers are stronger together, Cleo. You should know this by now." Will tells me and I nod my head in acceptance.

"Even when we don't technically have the last name Cooper, we're still stronger together. That's what being a family is all about. You can always count on Uncle Marcus, baby girl." I giggle through my tears and he winks at me.

"Have you spoken to Antony about all of this?" Nell asks gently and I shake my head.

"He knows about fucktwat. I haven't told him I'm scared of the press. That I was scared of being broken hearted around you guys, let alone in front of the world. That when he walks away from me I'll be devastated because I fucking love him more than I've ever loved anyone. And I won't get the chance now, will I? He isn't going to be waiting for me after that." I drop my head into my hands.

"I wouldn't be so sure about that." My head shoots up and my eyes are drawn by a magnetic pull toward the door, locking onto orbs the colour of whiskey.

"Sunflower, I walked away from you once and I promised myself I would never do it again. I told you, you're stuck with my brand of oddness for life, whether you like it or not. You can call that stalkerish, but I just call it love." He smiles at me and I jump up off my seat, flinging myself into his waiting arms.

"I'm so sorry. I love you. I never wanted you to doubt that. I want you. I want the forever kind with you but I'm still so scared." I cling to him as he wraps me in his arms and makes me feel safer than I've ever felt in my entire life.

"You have nothing to fear, *Girasole*. I'll never walk away from you. I haven't taken off this sunflower pin since the first time I put it on and I'm never taking it off. I'm never loving another woman again. I'm never kissing another woman. And I'm never going to stop asking you to be my wife. However long it takes, Cleopatra, *Mia Regina*. You will always be My Queen."

I press my lips to his and wrap my legs around his waist. He holds me in his arms and I cling to him like a baby monkey. I'm so grateful I haven't lost him. So grateful that he loves me and is willing to put the time and effort into us. I press kisses to his face, over his eyes, his lips, his cheeks and I don't stop until Princess declares, "If she ever moans about any of us and pda's again, I'm going to throat punch her."

Laughter erupts around us and, as my teeth start to chatter from the cold, Antony turns and walks us back into Nell's kitchen. A feeling of peace settles over me. I don't know if it's because I've explained everything to my family after so long or if it's because I'm finally starting to believe that Antony wants to be with me forever. Maybe it's both.

Regret swills inside of my head at saying no to marrying him. I want his ring on my finger and I want to be his wife, even if that means being spread on the front pages of the media. I know now that with my family and Antony by my side the press can't hurt me.

A plan starts to formulate in my head and I know exactly what to do to repay this amazing man for everything that he's given me. And I'm going to do it my way, the Cleo way.

CHAPTER 41

Antony

"I didn't expect you to be so fucking perky. I bought supplies for sad Antony. Had I known you were so fucking happy, I wouldn't have bothered. Why are you so happy?" Charlie asks me as he walks into my living room and finds me blaring music, singing along and doing my best Ed Sheeran impression with an invisible guitar.

"Cleopatra turned me down yesterday *but* we had a breakthrough. She finally opened up and actually told me what was going on with her. Her fears about the press and everything. And she opened up to her family too. Trust me, Bro, we've turned a corner." He rolls his eyes as I grin. "Plus, the scan results were really positive. Coach said I'll be back next season, so isn't replacing me. It's all good, Baby."

I follow him into the kitchen as he calls over his shoulder. "Please don't start calling me *'Baby'* again. It took years to get you to stop the last time. And you only did because Zoe asked you to." I chuckle at Charlie's ever-serious face and grab the bags of supplies off him. I dig inside, searching for the mint chocolate chip ice cream I know he's got for me.

"Bingo!" I shout and grab it out of the bag, holding it up like the world cup trophy. "You know I love you right now, don't you?" With a smile as gleeful as a kid at Christmas I spin around to grab a spoon, but my bounty is cruelly snatched from my hands. I turn back to Charlie and watch as he opens the lid and licks the entire top layer of the ice cream. With my eyes wide in shock and my mouth agape in horror I squawk loudly and full of pity, "Why?"

He continues to lick at it like it's a giant ice lolly as I stand immobile and affronted by his actions.

"This ice cream is for sad Antony, not Ed Sheeran-impersonating perky Antony. Sorry." He grins, his eyes shining mischievously.

I shake my head. "That's cold. Really cold. I expected more from you."

"You shouldn't. I licked this so it's mine." He tells me through a mouthful of *my* mint chocolate chip. I frown, drawing my eyebrows tightly together before laughing, grabbing a spoon, saying fuck it and digging into the ice cream.

"What the fuck, Dude? That's disgusting!" Charlie shouts as he throws the ice cream onto the counter.

"What?" I ask with my mouth filled with deliciousness.

"I licked it, Antony."

"So? What's the big deal? I've slept naked next to you and used your toothbrush before. Get a grip." I casually tell him as I bury more and more ice cream into my mouth, savouring the flavour dancing on my tongue and moaning at the taste.

"Stop making fucking sex noises whilst eating ice cream that's covered in my saliva. And what the fuck do you mean you've used my toothbrush? When? And when did you sleep naked next to me? I told you to always keep your boxers on. Fucking hell, Antony. You're a proper odd person." Charlie runs his hands through his hair and I cackle loudly at his disgust, causing me to spit ice cream all over the counter.

He shakes his head but his lips tip up at the corners and in moments he's grabbing the sides of the counter and belly laughing with me. Once the laughter subsides he grabs my spoon and takes a huge bite of the melting ice cream and says "may as well" as he shoves it into his mouth.

After we polish off the ice cream and tidy up the kitchen, Charlie casually asks me if I'd heard from my dad today.

"No, I'm actually a little annoyed to be honest. I tried phoning him but he didn't pick up. I texted him saying she said no this time and got a 'don't give up' text back but no phone call." I grab the cloth that we used to clean the spills of ice cream up and throw it into the sink.

"Don't stress about it. He phoned me earlier. Said something about not wanting to influence you with his 'Cleopatra ways' and you had to learn your own way."

I stand with my back against the sink and fold my arms over my chest. "Sounds like something he'd say. He thinks he has the monopoly on all Cleopatras. Fuck, I miss him. Can't wait to fly over and see him. I want him and Mama to meet Cleopatra, but not until she's ready. I was hoping they'd come to your party but Mama had another commitment that day. You're not important enough for her to cancel." I smirk.

He grins and I frown, not getting the reaction I expected off him. He grabs his wallet and keys and tells me, "I'm out, Marcello. Ciao, Baby."

CHAPTER 42

Cleo

My stomach is filled with dread. Sweat is dripping down my back and I have a smile pasted onto my face that I'm sure makes me look ridiculous. Not to mention the fucking costume Marcus made me wear that weighs a tonne and adds to my humiliation. Why I thought this was a good idea is beyond me.

"Because you realised you fucked up and wanted to make a huge statement to your unicorn, footballing, lover of love and all round oddball of a boyfriend." Emilia smirks, letting me know I must've been speaking out loud again.

"Shut up, Em-ili-aaa," I elongate her name on purpose to annoy her and snicker at the irritated twitch in her eye. "Why aren't you dressed up anyway? Everyone was supposed to be here with a plus one and dressed as a famous couple through the ages." I huff out as I fix the stupid bird crown thing that is supposed to sit regally on my head but is instead slipping down and trying to blind me.

"I am dressed up." She waves the toy gun she has in her hands and I study her 'costume.' Her long blonde hair is swept to the side in a braid and she has a fedora sitting prettily on her head. Her suit is black with white pinstripes on it and she wears a red flower in her lapel.

"As who? Al Capone?" I question her and blow a strand of hair out of my eyes. She sighs, shakes her head and places the toy gun on the ground, then reaches up and fixes my crown whilst I smile in relief.

"I'm Bonnie from Bonnie and Clyde. Marcus matches me. I couldn't come dressed as anything remotely fun or sexy because most of the attendees are my clients. Your headdress has a little clasp at the back. I attached it to your hair so it shouldn't move anymore. You look amazing, the party is fucking brilliant. Now relax and come out from back here."

I know she won't like it but I reach out and grab her into a cuddle. I wrap my arms around her tightly so she can't escape and feel her sigh against me. She lets her arms circle around me and squeezes me tightly too. A few seconds later we let go and pretend it never happened.

"I will. Everything is done back here now, and seeing as the magazine people have left I can get things rolling. Antony senior and Patti should be here soon. Zoe has arranged for them to be picked up from the hotel and brought here," I tell her whilst checking my clipboard to make sure everything is set.

"I still can't believe you got them over here. He will be so happy to see them." Emilia's eyes twinkle with pride.

"Charlie helped. I couldn't have done any of this without him. Or you." Emotion clogs my throat as I think about just how far I've come, and how many people were instrumental in helping me get here.

I wouldn't have been able to pull any of this together without them. Charlie managed to call Antony's parents before he did and explained that although I said no, I did in fact want to marry him. But I wanted to do it my way. His dad seemed to completely understand that and just chuckled about "Cleopatras" according to Charlie.

When I decided to propose to Antony, I knew I had to have everyone we love here. My mum and dad are in the crowd mingling about with masks on so Antony doesn't recognise them. Nell and Will are dressed as Oberon and Titania from *A Midsummer Night's Dream* and Connor and Juliet are Princess Buttercup and Westley. Antony hasn't seen my costume and doesn't know about anything I have planned.

I've watched from the sidelines as Zoe and Charlie have posed for pictures and had journalists asking pre-approved questions. I didn't even know that was something you could do, but after a very lengthy conversation with both Charlie and Emilia I've been schooled in the ways the press work. It seems Antony was right. He would have taken control of the situation and made sure any story was told in a truthful way.

It's what I'm doing. I've got the card of a journalist that Emilia has assured me is trustworthy and I've already booked us in for a meeting with her. Now all I have to do is propose in front of all the people we love most in the world and hope he says yes.

Emilia slaps my arm gently and it brings me back to the now. I nod my head in thanks.

"Go out there and find your Antony. You were made for this, Cleopatra."

I grin and square my shoulders, stepping out onto the stage to make my grand gesture to my handsome leading man.

CHAPTER 43

Antony

The party has been a massive success and Zoe and Charlie are the happiest I've ever seen them. I've been asked repeatedly by journalists and guests who I'm dressed as even though my roman gladiator costume should be a dead giveaway. I fiddle with the sunflower pin I managed to attach to the cape that swoops over my front and falls down my back. I haven't seen Cleopatra for the whole bloody event. She was supposed to be my plus one and I know she's working, but I wanted her with me tonight. She isn't dressed up, but technically we're still Antony and Cleopatra so we aren't breaking any rules. I dip my head at the sadness that starts to shadow my best friend's engagement party. It would've meant the world to me if she'd dressed up, but it's fine.

A slap to my shoulder brings my head up and I smirk when I catch sight of Brady and his friend Edie. "So I take it you're the big bad wolf and you're…" I look at his friend, wearing a skintight red dress with a hooded cape, her curves on display for everyone to see, and smirk when he clears his throat. "Little Red grew up, didn't she? I'm glad the wolf hasn't eaten you, Red."

She smirks at me and says, "Nope, he hasn't. Not yet

anyway." She winks at Brady, who splutters the drink he's just put into his mouth, and cackles loudly at the shocked expressions on both of our faces. "Sorry, Jaxy, I couldn't resist." She rubs his arm with her hand and bites on her bottom lip. Brady just stands frozen, watching her hand brush over his bicep, his breaths coming in short little pants. I excuse myself but I don't think either are aware of anyone or anything besides the raw sexual tension between them.

I spot Nell and William in the crowd and head over to them. "Hey guys. You having a good time? Didn't Cleopatra do an amazing job?"

Nell, with glassy eyes and rosy cheeks, lunges for me and embraces me in a hug whilst spilling wine all over her hand. "Oops, sh-orry, bro. Cleo is amazing. You're amazing, every-one'sh amazing and I can't wait to shee—"

"And that's enough for you, My lady. Let's get you some water," Will interrupts, snatching the glass from her hands. He unwraps her arms from my neck and wraps one around his shoulder.

"Hey, I was drunkin' that. Where are my shistas. Shistas. No, shistas. Yeah, Shistas." Nell slurs her way through her sentence and laughter spills out of my mouth.

"You're so pretty. Isn't he pretty?" she asks me whilst stroking Will's face. She drags her finger down his nose, to his mouth and drags his bottom lip out so it plops back again.

She starts to giggle and Will shakes his head and explains, "Sorry, she isn't used to drinking and is a tad bit drunk."

"As drunk-ded as a skunk-ded," Nell shouts excitedly as Juliet and Connor join us.

"Yes! I love drunk Nell. She's so much fun." Juliet exclaims.

Nell grins and attempts to high five herself and misses. She mumbles something about Juliet moving her hand away and tries again but misses again. "See, she's freaking hilarious," Juliet tells us as Nell tries to slap her own hand and misses again.

"And very chatty, Princess. Maybe you can help me steer her over to the bar for a glass of water." Will tilts his head away from me and Juliet nods, dragging Nell away and shushing her. I turn my confused gaze onto Connor who just grins.

"What?" I ask and watch as he shrugs his shoulders and the grin turns into a full blown smile as the lights for the stage go on and someone walks onstage. Connor chuckles next to me and I squint to see who's up there.

Through the lights, I can make out a figure. I'm just about to ask Connor who it is when the lights dim a bit and the breath is knocked right out from me. There, standing in the middle of the stage, looking like a beautiful Egyptian Queen and the other half of my soul, is my Cleopatra.

CHAPTER 44
Cleo

As the lights dim, I step toward the microphone. I take a deep breath and start to speak but I'm interrupted by Nell, drunkenly shouting, "Woo hoo shista. Woo hoo! Cleo, you a rockshtar and Alex ish a fucktwat—" I laugh as I spot Juliet tackle her to the ground and sit on top of her with her hand over her mouth.

"And that ladies and gents, was my big sister. She's not wrong. I am a rockstar and Alex is a fucksicle but that's neither here nor there." Laughter filters through the crowd and I take a deep breath before I continue.

"Many of you here know that my company organised this party." Various whoops and cheers ring out as I roll my eyes and grin at the same time. "Yeah, alright, pipe down will you? Footballers are rowdy fuckers," I tell them through a grin and get more cheers and whistles. My eyes scan the crowd and as soon as they lock onto the one person I was searching for that grin turns into a beaming smile.

I point at Antony and curl my finger into a 'come hither' motion and laugh as he runs through the crowd. "So I didn't plan this alone. I had a partner in all of this. Someone who decided to take it upon himself to sweep me off my feet and make me fall head over heels in love with his brand of oddness. Many of you know him as Marcello, but I know him as mine."

Antony barrels his way onto the stage and is met with cheers and cat calls. He wraps his arms around me and the crowd goes wild. I squeeze him tightly and inhale his scent but force myself to let him go. "You look amazing, Cleopatra." The microphone picks up his compliment and the crowd cheers again.

Laughing, I move the microphone so that it's in front of me. "I wanted to take this time, in front of all of Antony's nearest and dearest people, to tell you all how much I love him. Even if he did make me dress like this." I cut him a side-eyed look and he winks back. "He's the best person I've ever met, and if you'd met my family you'd know how much of a complement that is." I scan the crowd and see my parents, sisters, and the guys all making heart signs with their hands, except Nell who looks like she's passed out on Will's shoulder.

"Antony asked me a question the other day and I stupidly let fear get in the way of giving him the right answer." A waving couple catches my eye and I smile knowing that everything is now in place. "So, Antony, I wanted to tell you, I'm not afraid anymore. I'm taking control of my fears and making sure that they don't control me anymore. And with that I want to know if the offer to marry you is still on the table? If it is, I'd like to change my answer."

Antony takes my hand and smiles. "Of course it fucking is Cleopatra." He says it so loudly he's heard across the party without the microphone.

"Antony, don't swear." A voice calls out.

"Sorry Mama." Antony remarks casually. Then realisation hits and he slowly blinks as his mouth drops open in shock. "Mama?" He turns to me, then the crowd, and as the spotlight hits his parents, he laughs as he realises who they came dressed as. "We already have Antony and Cleopatra covered, you guys need to change."

Laughter fills the room and Antony Senior calls back, "*Mio figlio*, we are the original Antony and Cleopatra, you two can be the understudies. Now propose properly so I can give my daughter-in-law a kiss, will you?"

With a beaming grin, Antony turns back to me and starts to kneel but I stop him, "A king mustn't kneel Antony, *Il mio re.*"

He brings his eyes to mine, smiles and whispers, "*Mia regina.* Cleopatra, will you marry me?"

There's a collective gasp from the crowd and I chuckle as I answer, "Yes. I want the forever kind with you, Antony."

He cups my cheek in his hand and lowers his mouth to mine and murmurs, "Sunflower" against my lips.

His kiss starts off slow and sweet but within seconds the hunger splices through the both of us. I groan as his tongue caresses mine and he moans into my mouth. My hand snakes up and into his hair until a loud "A-hem" brings us out of our lust addled minds. I giggle as Antony Senior stands next to us on the stage and laugh loudly when Marcus, who is standing behind Antony, shouts over to me, "Get it, baby girl."

Antony crushes me against him and I sigh as his warmth, his scent, his love, engulfs me. This man who drove me mad, made me hornier than I've ever been, and made me fall deeply in love with his brand of oddness, is mine. And I want everyone to know it.

I know he isn't going anywhere. I know we will be okay. Because we have the forever kind, and that's not a fleeting feeling.

Epilogue

ANTONY

It's been six months since Cleopatra proposed to me on stage, or told me to propose to her on stage. I don't even know who proposed to who and I don't care. All I care about is that Cleopatra and I are engaged and are planning our wedding for next year. It won't be an extravagant affair, but it will be in Italy with all of our loved ones there to witness it.

I haven't been able to convince her to move out of London yet but I have convinced her to move into my house. It took a long time, but I finally managed to get her to agree, only on the condition that Marcus took over her apartment.

He was hesitant when she told him, but then almost wet himself with excitement. "You're telling me, I get to live downstairs from my Boo? In an apartment that is absolutely stunning and is as cheap as anything and there's no catch? Nothing? This isn't a joke? Verity isn't going to come home and demand her apartment back without any notice or anything like that?" he'd demanded. And when Cleopatra convinced him everything was on the up and up, he squealed for what seemed like an hour. My Sunflower and I politely, and with great difficulty, held in our laughter when he told us, "Oh my ducking God, Baby girl, you are officially my favourite Cooper. Please don't tell Emilia I said that, she will maim me. But seriously, you, I ducking love you so much! Antony, thank you for making her fall in love with you and give me this beautiful apartment." He then proceeded to grab me in a hug that was so tight I thought I was going to lose consciousness.

As we load the final box into the removal van I grin at her. "That's it. Everything you own is in this van and will soon be on its way to our house. How do you feel, Sunflower?"

She smiles up at me from the floor of the van with her legs crossed. "I'm so tired. My whole body is screaming at me to stop moving now. As soon as we get home, I'm taking a nap."

I reach down and grab her hands, pulling her into a standing position, and push her up against the side of the van with her hands clasped over her head.

"You know what calling it home does to me, Cleopatra. It makes me get all excited now, doesn't it?" I grind my erection into her and she purrs against me. "You still thinking of taking a nap as soon as we get home, Sunflower?"

I bring my lips to her neck, biting and kissing my way up to her mouth. She shakes her head as I smirk against her cheek.

"What will you be doing then, Cleopatra?" She gasps as my other hand finds her nipple and rolls it through her shirt.

"You, Antony. I'll be doing you."

I growl and smash my lips onto hers. The taste of her sends a fire raging through my body. The urge to consume her overpowers me. I need to have this woman and I'll need her for the rest of our lives. Our teeth clash together as our lips and tongues frantically fight for control of the kiss. My senses are overwhelmed with her. I can smell her, taste her, feel her, and hear her groans. It's like I'm drunk on her. The all consuming being that is my sunflower.

She pushes against my hand holding hers in place and I nip at her bottom lip in warning. But before I can reinforce who's in control, who owns her soul, the van door swings open and her sister's disgusted face fills the doorway.

Emilia rolls her eyes and shakes her head but I can see the corners of her lips tipping up into a smile as well. She fights to stop it but finally lets the smile overtake her face for a second. I grin and she rolls her eyes again. I can't help the overwhelming love I have for these Coopers who accepted me into their lives so freely, but especially Emilia. From the very beginning she's rooted for me, helped me when things looked impossible, and out of all of them I have a special bond with her.

"Oh, hey guys." Cleopatra says casually but the squeakiness in her voice gives away her embarrassment.

As Emilia laughs at our expense and I subtly rearrange my dick to give it some much needed room, another box is loaded onto the van. I turn my attention away from Cleopatra and look at who threw it on the pile. "I thought we got them all. Thanks for all your help, man, really appreciate it." I jump down and out of the van and offer my hand out to shake his and he clasps it with a smile on his face.

"No problem, bro. What's family for?" he asks me and smirks in Emilia's direction as her eyes glower at him, a sight that would normally make a grown man quake in his boots. His smirk turns into a grin the longer she glares at him.

"You're not family," she spits out through gritted teeth and he laughs at her.

He holds up his left hand and points to the platinum band on his ring finger. "This says differently, Angel." She glares at him but he continues to laugh until she eventually stomps off into her building.

"You're not going to win her over like that," Cleopatra warns him as she jumps off the van and stands next to me.

"I know but she's so much fun to irritate." He chuckles, salutes us, and follows her.

The man is brave, I'll give him that much. Messing with the Shark is a dangerous thing to do, but if anyone can win against her, it's him.

I look into the van and smile when I spot Cleopatra's easel propped up against the boxes. I can't wait for her to see the surprise I have in store. I've turned one of our spare rooms into an art studio. I've ordered new paints, easels, canvases in various shapes and sizes, and I've decorated it with sunflowers everywhere. I hope she loves it and I really hope she paints some more pictures for us to put up in our home too.

Everyone loves her paintings. I know Nell has requested a Cleopatra original, as has Connor and my mama too. I especially love the one with red hearts, sunflowers and brown eyes, but mainly because when she painted it I was in her head without her knowing it. We were meant to be.

"You ready to go home, Baby?" Cleopatra asks innocently, but I see the twinkle of mischief in her eyes. I grin back and let her see all the emotions flash across my face. The want, the need. She can feel the love that's coursing through my veins for her every second of the day.

"You bet your sweet arse I am." As she spins away from me giggling, I give her backside a slap. She turns to look over her shoulder and bites her bottom lip. Desire flashes through her eyes. I growl and throw her over my shoulder, shoving her into the front of the van. Her giggles are floating through the air as we move. The sooner I get her home, the sooner we can start our odd forever kind of life together.

THE END

Acknowledgments

It's funny. With every book I write I get to this part and always feel like I've run out of words. That everything I want to say has already been said. And I suppose it has but I'm going to say it again anyway.

THANK YOU! To everyone who has read any of my books, ever, thank you. It really does mean the world to me and I'm forever grateful.

To my family, thank you for putting up with me talking about characters as if they were real people and confusing you one to many times, I'm sorry. But in my defence they are real in my head, especially Marcus when he sings his own version of the Macarena and makes new dance moves up to go with it.

To my Dream Team, you guys are amazing. Your memes make me laugh out loud and always cheer me up. I love how interactive you all are with each other and me. Don't ever change. As always, like jelly tots, FOREVER!

Thank you to Michelle and the stalker sisters for always being there to lend a helping hand and offer support and encouragement. You really are the kindest and best people and I can't wait to meet you all in person next year.

Thank you to Valerie. My voice of reason, my book bestie and my sister from another mister. I love you.

Thank you, all of you, for taking a little unknown author under your wing and falling in love with these crazy sisters. My heart is bursting with love and pride. You all mean more to me than you know and I love you all lots, like jelly tots xxxx

About the Author

Koko Heart is a romance writer who lives in London, United Kingdom, with her husband and their four daughters. She writes from her heart and has always been fascinated with happily ever afters. She still believes in fairytales but likes them a little bit dirtier now.

Also by Koko Heart

Mine, always - Amazon and KU

Mine, finally - https://dl.bookfunnel.com/4um95dy6pa

A book funnel freebie

The Cooper Sisters Series:

I'm all yours - Amazon and KU

Till this night - Amazon and KU

The forever kind - Amazon and KU

Book four - Emilia's story is coming later this year

Book five - Marcus's novella is coming later this year too

Sign up to my mailing list for all the latest news on releases and what's coming next here: https://subscribepage.io/fvdMPN

Printed in Great Britain
by Amazon

22155897R00139